New York Times *bestselling author LaVyrle Spencer, who* "*knows how to tug at readers' heartstrings*" (Publishers Weekly), *offers here one of her most beloved stories—about a woman who must look past the surface to see true beauty within . . .*

Allison Scott has her mind on her career. As an up-and-coming photographer, she has neither the time nor the inclination for an affair—especially since her last attempt at love, with a handsome model of hers, left her once bitten, twice shy. Now she keeps a wary eye out for beautiful men. But Rick Lang, who only models to pay the bills, can see through Allison's aloofness to the aching heart beneath. And he's determined to prove that he's one handsome man who can be trusted with the gift of her love . . .

"Spencer . . . leaves the reader breathless."
—*New York Daily News*

"Spencer is a winner."
—*San Antonio Express-News*

continued . . .

THE BESTSELLING NOVELS OF LAVYRLE SPENCER

Then Came Heaven
A triumphant story of faith and love . . . "Touching."
—*Chattanooga Times*

Small Town Girl
A country-music star rediscovers her heart . . . "Warm and folksy." —*Kirkus Reviews*

That Camden Summer
A shunned divorcée finds unexpected love . . . "A modern fairy tale." —*People*

Home Song
A secret threatens to tear a family apart . . . "Tug[s] at readers' heartstrings." —*Publishers Weekly*

Family Blessings
A widow is torn between her family and new love . . . "A moving tale." —*Publishers Weekly*

November of the Heart
True love blooms for two hearts from different worlds . . . "One of Spencer's best." —*Kirkus Reviews*

Bygones
A moving story of a family at a crossroads . . . "A page-turner." —*New York Daily News*

Forgiving
A beautiful story of family ties renewed . . . "A lively story." —*New York Daily News*

Bitter Sweet
The poignant tale of high school sweethearts reunited . . . "A journey of self-discovery and reawakening." —*Booklist*

The Endearment

A woman's love is threatened by past secrets . . . "A tender, sensual story."   —Lisa Gregory

Morning Glory

Two misfit hearts find tenderness . . . "A superb book."
—New York Daily News

Spring Fancy

A bride-to-be falls in love—with another man . . . "Incredible beauty."   —Affaire de Coeur

The Hellion

Sparks fly between a lady and a hell-raiser . . . "Superb."
—Chicago Sun-Times

Vows

Two willful lovers—one special promise . . . "Magic."
—Affaire de Coeur

The Gamble

Take a chance on love . . . "Grand."   —Good Housekeeping

Years

Across the Western plains, only the strongest survived . . . "Splendid."   —Publishers Weekly

Separate Beds

First came the baby, then marriage . . . then love . . . "A superb story."   —Los Angeles Times

Twice Loved

A woman's missing husband returns—after she's remarried . . . "Emotional."   —Rocky Mountain News

Hummingbird

The novel that launched LaVyrle Spencer's stunning career . . . "Will leave you breathless."   —Affaire de Coeur

Titles by LaVyrle Spencer

FORSAKING ALL OTHERS
THEN CAME HEAVEN
SMALL TOWN GIRL
THAT CAMDEN SUMMER
HOME SONG
FAMILY BLESSINGS
NOVEMBER OF THE HEART
BYGONES
FORGIVING
BITTER SWEET
THE ENDEARMENT
MORNING GLORY
SPRING FANCY
THE HELLION
VOWS
THE GAMBLE
A HEART SPEAKS
YEARS
SEPARATE BEDS
TWICE LOVED
SWEET MEMORIES
HUMMINGBIRD
THE FULFILLMENT

Forsaking All Others

LaVYRLE SPENCER

JOVE BOOKS, NEW YORK

FORSAKING ALL OTHERS

A Jove Book / published by arrangement with
the author

PRINTING HISTORY
First Jove mass-market edition / October 1982
Second Jove mass-market edition / December 2003

Copyright © 1982 by LaVyrle Spencer
Cover design by Oysterpond Group
Book design by Kristin del Rosario

For information address: The Berkley Publishing Group,
a division of Penguin Group (USA) Inc.,
375 Hudson Street, New York, New York 10014.

ISBN: 0-515-13700-6

A JOVE BOOK®
Jove Books are published by The Berkley Publishing Group,
a division of Penguin Group (USA) Inc.,
375 Hudson Street, New York, New York 10014.
JOVE and the "J" design
are trademarks belonging to Penguin Group (USA) Inc.

PRINTED IN THE UNITED STATES OF AMERICA

10 9 8 7 6 5 4 3 2 1

With love to
my friend
Dorothy Garlock

Chapter
ONE

NORTH Star Agency," answered the voice on the phone.

Allison Scott crossed her ankles, rested a heel on her desk, and leaned back in her ancient, creaking swivel chair. "I need the sexiest man you've ever seen and I need him right now," she said, smiling.

"Hey, who doesn't?" came the glib reply. "Allison, is that you?"

"Yes, Mattie, it's me, and I mean it. I need the man to end all men. He's got to be handsome, honed, with hair the color of waving wheat, blue eyes—but I could get by with brown—a jaw like Dick Tracy's and a nose like the hand of a sundial, a body like—"

"Hey, hey, hey! Hold on there, girl. What are you using him for anyway, a screen test?"

"Not quite. A book cover."

"A what!"

"A book cover." Allison's voice became exhilarated. "I got the offer about a month ago, and I said I'd see what I thought after reading the book. It came in yesterday's mail, and I took it home last night, read it from cover to cover, and decided to give it a try. I just called New York and—oh, Mattie, this could be the break I've been waiting for. They'll be sending a contract within the week. Now all I need from you is Mister Right for the cover."

"Let me get his vital stats on paper and look through the files and see what I can come up with. Okay, shoot."

Allison's feet hit the floor as she reached for the manuscript, flipped to the right page, and followed the words with her finger. "Blond, blue eyed, virile, handsome, about twenty-five years old, six feet, sinewy . . . God, Mattie, can you believe they really believe men who look like that are worth anything?" Allison slapped the manuscript closed in disgust.

Mattie's voice came back critically. "Were you hired as a book critic or cover artist?"

"All right, I deserved that. It's really none of my business what these star-struck authors put between the covers. This is a chance I've been waiting for, and if they want me to give them a picture that'll convince the readers people fall in love at first sight and live happily ever after, that's what I'll give 'em. You just send me the raw material and watch me!"

"Okay. So describe the woman."

"Ah, let's see . . ." Again a slender finger scanned a page. "Oh, here it is. Early twenties, ginger-colored hair, blue eyes, tall, willowy. And listen, Mattie, hair color is important, seems the readers tend to notice if it's wrong, so shoulder length and ginger, right?"

"Ginger it is. Let me see what I can dig up, and I'll get the photos over to you in tomorrow's mail."

"Okay, Mattie, I appreciate it."

"Hey, Allison?"

"Yeah?"

A brief silence hummed before Mattie asked guardedly, "Is he back yet?"

Allison Scott's back wilted. Her elbow dropped to the desk, and she rubbed her forehead as if to ease a sudden shooting pain. "No, he's not. I'm really not expecting him anymore, Mattie."

"Have you heard from him?"

"Not a word."

Allison thought she could hear Mattie sigh. "I'm sorry I asked. Forgive me, huh?"

Allison sighed herself. "Mattie, it's not your fault Jason Ederlie turned out to be a first-class bastard."

"I know it, but I shouldn't have asked."

"My skin's gotten a lot tougher since he disappeared."

"I know that, too. That's what worries me."

"What do you mean by that!"

Mattie backed off at Allison's sharp tone. "Nothing. Forget I said it, okay? The glossies will be in tomorrow's mail."

The click at the other end of the line ended any further questions Allison might have posed, but her ebullient mood was gone, snuffed away at the mention of Jason Ederlie's name. Pushing his memory aside, she swiveled abruptly, rocked to her feet, and thrust belligerent hands deep into the pockets of her khaki-colored jeans. Standing with feet spread, she stared out the ceiling-to-floor windows that overlooked downtown Minneapolis. The building was old and drafty but spacious and bright, thus well suited for a photography studio. At one time it had housed the offices of a flour-milling company that had long ago turned to carpets, subdued lighting, well-insulated walls, and piped-in music.

But as Allison stared out unseeingly, the only music she heard was that of aged water pipes overhead, the clang of the expanding metal in ancient radiators that heated the place—but never quite adequately, it seemed.

The January cold had condensed moisture on the north-facing panes. Now and then a rivulet streamed down and joined the drift of ice that had formed at the corners of the small panes. With the edge of a clenched fist Allison cleared the center of a square, but the view beyond remained foggy.

Her fist slid down the cold glass, then rapped hard against an icy frame.

"Damn you, Jason, damn you!" she exclaimed aloud. Her forehead fell to her arm and tears trickled down her cheek as she indulged in the memory of his face, his voice, his body, all those things she had learned to trust.

Abruptly her head jerked up and she tossed it defiantly, sending her hair flying back in a rusty swirl of obstinance. She dragged the back of one wrist across her nose, sniffed, dashed the errant tears from her eyes, and swallowed the lump of memory in her throat. "I'll get over you, Jason Ederlie, if it's the last thing I do!" she promised the empty studio, the skyline, herself. Then Allison Scott turned back to the balm of work.

IT was a simple book, an uncomplicated story of a man and woman who meet on vacation on Sanibel Island, look at each other while sparks fly, make their way into each other's arms within fifty pages, out of them by a hundred, right their misconceptions some fifty pages later, and regain bliss together as the book ends. Perhaps because the hero's description matched that of Jason Ederlie, Allison had found herself lost in the pages.

Maybe that, too, was the reason she'd at first been reluctant to accept the contract to do the cover art, for without Jason to pose, something would be missing. But realizing what a boon it would mean to her career and her finances, she'd accepted, even though it galled Allison that women readers sopped up such Cinderellaism as if it really happened.

Allison Scott knew better. Cinderella endings were found only in paperback romances on the shelves of the grocery store.

At the end of the day, reaching for a can of spaghetti and meatballs at the PDQ Market, she felt the bluntness of that fact all too fully, for she hated the thought of walking into the emptiness awaiting her at home, now that Jason was gone.

Home. She thought about the word as she drove from downtown Minneapolis around "the lakes," as they were loosely called. There were five of them—Calhoun, Harriet, Nokomis, Lake of the Isles, and Cedar—forming the heart of the beautiful "City of the Lakes." Allison lived on the west side of Lake of the Isles, in a second-story apartment in a regal old house that had been well preserved since the turn of the century.

She could barely see the first-floor windows as she turned in the driveway and threaded her Chevy van to the detached garage at the rear, for the snow had been inordinately heavy this year, and the banks beside the drive were shoulder high. She closed the garage door and glanced at the frozen surface of the lake. Shivering, she tucked her chin deep into the collar of her warm jacket as she headed for the private stairway running up the outside of the house.

Home. She turned the key but dreaded going in, a feeling she'd been unable to overcome during the last six weeks. As she moved inside and shut the door on the subzero temperature, her eyes scanned the living room that she'd carefully decorated to bring a little bit of summer into the Minnesota winters—gleaming hardwood floors, the old kind they don't lay any more; the Scandinavian import rug she'd searched so long to find, with its clever blending of greens, yellow, and white in an unimposing oblique swirl of design; airy rattan and wicker furniture with fat cushions of a green-and-yellow print that brought to mind warm, tropical rain forests; a multitude of potted palms, scheffleras, philodendrons, and more, flourishing on windowsills, tables, and on a small white stepladder in front of four long, narrow windows; lime-and-white Roman shades of woven wood that added to the tropical air; a pair of French doors leading to the summer sun porch over-looking the lake; a hanging lamp with a white wicker shade that matched the floor lamp behind her favorite renovated wicker rocker with its rolled arms and thick pillows. And everywhere an impression of light and space.

Yes, it was like a breath of summer. Oh, how she'd loved this place . . . until Jason.

But now whenever she returned it was only to remember him here, slouched in the enfolding basket chair that hung from the ceiling, in one corner, his heel resting on the floor as he made the thing go wiggly-waggly, all the while teasing her with those gorgeous grinning eyes or that sensuous pair of lips that photographed like no others she'd ever caught in her viewfinder.

Jason . . . Jason . . . he was everywhere. Leaning over his morning coffee at the glass-topped dining table with its chrome-and-wicker chairs, often as not with one leg thrown over a chair arm, foot bare, swinging in time to the music he always seemed to hear in his head, whether it was playing on the stereo or not. Jason . . . sprawled diagonally across the squeaky old bed, studying the ceiling with fingers entwined behind his neck, talking about making it big. Jason . . . digging through the clothing that had hung beside hers in the closet, searching for just the right look that'd finally catch some producer's eye. Jason . . . blow-drying his razor-cut hair in the bathroom, nothing but a towel twisted around his hips, whistling absently as she leaned against the doorway watching him . . . just watching. Jason . . . spread-eagled on the living room floor, teasing, tempting, while

8

The Five Senses sang, "When I'm stretched on the floor after loving once more, with your skin pressing mine, and we're tired and fine. . . ."

Jason, with the face and body of Adonis. It had never ceased to amaze Allison that he should have chosen such an ordinary looking girl as herself. He was beauty personified, a spellbinding combination of muscle, grace, and facial symmetry that spoke as poignantly to the artist in Allison Scott as to the woman in her. With Jason before the camera there could be no poor shots—his face wasn't capable of being captured at an unflattering angle. So while she'd had him, business had soared. Sport coats, leather goods, candy bars, road machinery—it seemed there was no product Jason's face could not sell, or so thought Twin Cities ad agencies.

Meanwhile, the portfolio of photos grew, and they made plans for a fashion layout in *Gentlemen's Review* magazine. It had been Allison's dream. But to sell to *GR*, to even approach them, Allison needed between three and four thousand photos. So she shot him everywhere, in every light, in every pose, against every background, learning with each click of the shutter to love him more.

And then six weeks ago she'd returned home to find half the closet empty, the razor gone from the bathroom, a damp towel over the sink, and the entire collection of negatives gone, too, and along with them, her dreams. He had left one thing—their favorite photo of him, blown up to poster size, on the four-foot easel in the living room. Across the bottom of it he had scrawled, "Sorry, babe . . . Love, Jason."

The easel stood now at the far end of the room, in the opposite corner from the hanging basket chair. Its pegs were empty, for when Allison had finally admitted that Jason wasn't coming back, she'd taken that overblown ego symbol, with all its memories, and stuffed it behind a bunch of unsold works stacked against the bedroom wall. She could hide the photo, but it seemed she could not hide the hurt. For it was back as keen as ever, resurrected by a simple thing like a two-dollar romance for which she'd agreed to do the cover.

Only she needed Jason to do it.

She turned away, toward the small kitchen alcove where she heated the spaghetti and ate it standing up, leaning against the kitchen cabinet, for she dreaded sitting at the table alone with Jason's image shimmering again as if he were still there, opposite her, as he'd been for the better part of a year.

Damn that story! Damn that hero who had to bring Jason's memory back all fresh and vibrant! Damn Mattie and her innocent questions!

The spaghetti tasted like wallpaper paste, but it filled the hole, and that's all Allison cared about anymore. Mealtimes were to be endured now, not savored as when there'd been the two of them together.

The way the apartment was arranged there was little

to distinguish where the kitchen stopped and the dining area began. They ran together, then on to become the living room. Leaning now against the cabinets with a kettle in one hand and a fork in the other, Allison studied the empty easel, wondering where he was, who he was with, if he was modeling again. As tears filled her eyes, she thought: Damn you, Jason Ederlie, if you ever come back expecting to find your gorgeous face and body still haunting me from the corner of the living room, you'll be sadly disappointed!

But the fork dropped into the kettle, the kettle into the sink, and her head onto her arms as despair and regret welled up in her throat.

THE following day was one of those grim efforts to make a living. Working with a pre-set camera, Allison spent six hours taking elementary-school pictures of gap-toothed second-graders, measuring the distance from camera to nose with the string that dangled from the tripod. It wasn't art, but it paid the rent on the studio.

By three o'clock in the afternoon, when the school session finished, the temperature was already dropping outside. Allison pulled a fat, fuzzy bobcap low over her forehead, wound a matching scarf twice around her neck, and headed for the van and downtown.

The ice on the studio windows was thick, the floor

drafty. But the promised portfolio of glossies was in the mail. A quick check with the answering service turned up nothing needing immediate attention, so Allison headed home, her spirits a little higher than they'd been yesterday when she'd faced the empty apartment.

She made a cup of hot cocoa, slammed a tape into the tapedeck, and curled up against the puffy pillows of the sofa to see what Mattie had come up with.

Inside the mustard-colored envelope was a note in Mattie's writing: "Sorry they're not all in color, but I pulled some that looked as if coloring would be right. Love, M."

The girls came first, a bevy of fifteen faces, some in color, some in black and white, all with shoulder-length hair, as requested. One by one she laid them on the end table and against the cushions of the sofa. Some of the faces were passable, but none bowled Allison over. Semi-perturbed, she started looking through the men.

A smiling face with one tooth slightly crooked, giving an appealing little-boy look. Another with a sober aspect that somehow lacked character. Next, a glamour boy whose face was handsome enough but who somehow made Allison sure he wouldn't have any hair on his chest—for the poses she had planned, that was important. Next came a rugged type who'd adapt well to a Stetson and cigar.

But when the rugged type fell face down with the others, the cup of cocoa stopped halfway to Allison's lips, her eyes became riveted, and her back came away from the pillows. For a long moment she only stared, then her hand brought the cup toward her lips, and the next thing she knew, she'd burned her tongue.

"Ouch, dammit!" Depositing the cup and saucer on the glass-topped coffee table, she rose to her feet, scattering male faces from lap to floor as she held the single, striking face at arm's length.

"Holy cow," she breathed, stricken. "Holy ... holy ... cow." The face seemed too perfect to be flesh, the hair too disorderly to be accidental, the eyes so warm they seemed to reflect the change beneath the light from the table lamp. The nose was straight, with gorgeous nostrils. He had long cheeks and a strong jaw. And the mouth—ah, what a mouth. She studied it as an artist, but reacted as a woman.

The upper lip was utter perfection, its outline crisp, bowed with two peaks into perfect symmetry—a rare thing, no matter what the untutored layman might think. The lower lip was fuller than the upper, and the half smile seemed to hint at amusing things on his mind. Flat ears, strong neck—but not too thick—good shoulders, one leaning at an angle into the picture. He wore what appeared to be a wrinkled dress shirt with its collar askew, not the customary satin showman's costume, nor what Allison had come to think of as the "Tom Jones

Look"—open-necked shirt plunging low underneath a body-hugging, open suit jacket. Still, she smiled.

I'll bet any money there'll be hair on his chest, she thought.

Allison flipped the picture over.

Richard Lang . . . 4-11-57 . . . blond . . . blue.

She read the words again, and somehow they didn't seem enough. Richard Lang . . . 4-11-57 . . . blond . . . blue. God, was that all they had to say about a face like this? Who was he? Why hadn't she ever seen his photo in the North Star files before? He had the kind of features photographers dream of. Bone structure that created angles and hollows, beautiful for shadowing. The jaw and chin seemed to be living, the mouth made for mobility. She imagined it scowling, smiling, scolding. She wondered if it were as mobile in real life as it seemed on paper. Something said "dimples" when there actually were none, only attractive smile lines on either side of his mouth, as if smiling came easily.

Richard Lang.

Twenty-five years old, blond hair, blue eyes, face as captivating as . . . but Allison stopped herself just short of finishing, "Jason's."

Richard Lang, you're the one!

She leaned the eight-by-ten glossy against the base of a table lamp and backed off, studying it while she unbuttoned her cuffs, then the buttons up the front of her shirt. She reached for her cup, took it a reasonable distance away while blowing and sipping, and studied the face, already posing him, figuring the camera angles, the lighting, the background, which could not be too involved lest it detract from that face.

There wasn't a girl in the lot pretty enough for him. The girl, she could see, was going to give her trouble. It had been made clear to Allison that in the photograph the hero must appear to be overcome by the heroine, yet that was going to be hard to do with a face like his! It would overshadow any other within a country mile!

Allison, you're getting carried away.

To bring Richard Lang back into perspective, Allison deposited her empty cup in the sink, clumped into the bedroom, flung off her shirt, squirmed out of her jeans, and snuggled into a blue, fleecy robe, thinking all the while that when she returned to the living room she'd find the flaw she must have overlooked.

But he leaned there against the base of the lamp, more handsome than she'd remembered, making her hand move in slow motion as she zipped up the front of her robe.

She wished the photo was in color. Maybe his skin wasn't as clear as the black and white made it appear. Maybe he had freckles, ruddiness, sallow coloring. But she somehow knew his skin would be as smooth and healthy as a lifeguard's. Still searching for flaws, she thought maybe he has a horrible temper. Catching herself, she scolded, well, what does that matter, Allison Scott! You're taking his photo, not his name. If he has the temperament of a weasel, it's no affair of yours!

Nevertheless, it was hard to sleep that night. She hadn't been this exhilarated about her work since Jason had left.

The following morning she called Mattie to request more glossies of girls, and the two agreed to meet for lunch. Over steaming bowls of chicken-and-dumpling soup at Peter's Grill, Allison found herself hungry— actually hungry!—for the first time in weeks.

When Mattie asked which male model she'd chosen, Allison produced the photo of Richard Lang and laid it on the table between them.

"Him!" Mattie pointed a stubby finger. "I knew it! I knew he was the one you'd pick. All I had to hear was blond and blue, and I had him pegged in a second. He's just the type you can do wonders with on film."

"I'm sure as hell going to try, Mattie," Allison said thoughtfully. Then, studying the photo, struck again by his perfection, she asked, "What do you know about him?"

"Not much. He doesn't seem to give a fig leaf for what he wears. The times I've seen him he's been in battered-up tennies, washed out blue jeans, and wrinkled shirts that look like no woman ever touched an iron to them. Kind of strange, since most of our clients tend to overdo it when they dress for a booking."

"Mmm . . . so I noticed. His shirt looks like it's been through the Hundred Years War, and his hair . . . lord, Mattie, would you look at that hair! It's . . . it's . . ."

"Natural," Mattie finished.

"Yeah." Allison cocked her head and eyed the photo. "Natural, just like the rest of him. I wonder what the giant flaw is going to be when I get a look at him in person."

"Probably ego, like most of the pretty boys we handle."

The thought was depressing. "Probably," Allison agreed, stuffing the picture away again. "You don't have to teach me about ego in male models. Not after Jason Ederlie."

"I'm sorry I brought him up yes—"

"No, Mattie, it's okay." Allison held up her palms. "If I can't be adult enough to accept his being gone, I shouldn't have invited him to move in in the first place without any commitments on either side. It was . . . it was an idyll, a dream. But it's over, and I'm done licking my wounds. I'm going to throw myself into my work and make a name for myself, and when it's made I'll choose the man I want to live with, he won't choose me."

"Well, when you do, honey, why don't you make him a nice, stable plumber or grocer or accountant? Somebody who smiles at more than just himself in the mirror."

"Don't worry, Mattie. I've learned my lesson. When I find him, he'll be generous, humble, and honorable, and he'll dote upon my every desire."

LaVYRLE SPENCER

Mattie laughed. "Hey, wherever you find him, could you pick up two—one for me?"

They laughed together, Mattie in her size sixteen slacks and Allison with her shattered illusions. But in the end Allison wondered if such men existed.

Chapter
TWO

THE old Genesis Building had two elevators, one for passengers and one for freight. Naturally the old relics were both out of order when Allison got there, so she was totally out of breath as she unlocked the studio door after climbing six flights of stairs.

The phone was shrilling, and she tore across the room to grab it, puffing breathlessly as she answered, "Ph . . . Photo Images."

"Hello, this is Rick Lang. I was told to call this number, that you may possibly have a booking for me over there."

"Rick . . . L . . ." Suddenly the light dawned. "Oh! *Richard* Lang! The one in the photo from North Star's files."

"Right, but I go by Rick."

Allison was caught off guard by the pleasant, unaffected voice on the other end. It was deep, masculine, and easy. If she was looking for shortcomings in the man, his voice wasn't offering any clues.

"Rick . . . all right. Listen, I never make decisions from photos alone. I'd like to see you before we sign any contracts, okay?"

"Sure, that's understandable."

The image of his face came back to Allison, suddenly making her feel like a damn fool for insisting. What could she possibly find wrong with a face like that?

"Please understand, I'll be relying heavily on this job to bring in other similar work. If there's anything about you that—"

"Hey, sure, I understand. Sometimes black-and-whites can be misleading."

Of all things, Allison felt herself blushing. Blushing! Talking on the phone clear across a city where he couldn't even see her, she was stammering and blushing while he maintained perfect poise.

"When are you free?"

"I'm my own man. When would you like to see me?"

"How about tomorrow at one o'clock?"

"Fine."

"Can you come up to my studio?"

"Sure, if you tell me how to get there." She gave him instructions on where to park and what to do if the creaking old elevator was still balking, and more careful instructions on what to do if it wasn't. She heard his laughter then for the first time, a light, mirthful enjoyment in deep tones, before he ended, "I'll see you at one o'clock, then."

When she'd wished him good-bye, she fell back into her swivel chair, linked her fingers and hung her palms on the top of her head. This was ridiculous. She was becoming paranoid, looking for faults in him even before she met him, hoping to hear an effeminate tone in his voice, poor grammar, a lisp . . . something!

Scott, get your ass going! she chided, and jumped to her feet. He's not Jason, and he's not going to move in with you, so call a sand-and-gravel company and get a promise of free sand in exchange for free publicity shots of their operation or free photos of the owner's grandchildren or whatever it takes to get that sand up here. But get your mind off Rick Lang!

T HE following afternoon, Rick Lang entered the door of Photo Images to find a woman with her back to him, talking on the phone. She was tilted far back in an ancient oak swivel chair, the high heel of one brown leather boot propped high onto a frame of a huge wall of windows, the other ankle crossed over her knee. Spicy brown hair hung to her shoulder blades, held behind her ears by a pair of oversized sunglasses pushed onto the top of her head. His eyes followed the taut blue jeans on the outstretched leg, took in a bulky gray sweater and a coordinated woolen scarf wrapped twice around her neck. Suddenly she gestured at the ceiling like an Italian fruit vendor haggling over the price of an apple.

"But what if I sign up and get the bends or something, can I get my money back?" She gestured again, more exasperatedly, and the foot that rested on the knee started tapping the air sideways. Rick stood there, smiling, listening. The foot stopped tapping, the chin came down. "Oh, you can't?" she asked. "Not in a swimming pool?" She lowered the sunglasses to their proper place, and her voice turned innocent. "Well, to tell the truth, I really don't want to learn to scuba." She scratched the blue denim on her knee, nervously. "I just needed to use the gear for a couple of days for a photo project I'm planning and—"

She yanked the phone away from her ear, while across the room Rick heard snatches of a man's angry reply. "Lady . . . every curious . . . try diving . . . out of business . . . no time . . . want lessons."

The chair rocked forward, and her boots hit the floor with a slap. "Well, you don't have to get so—" She stopped, cut off, listened a moment longer, then spit, "Mister, I'm not after free—" Again she listened, then abruptly slammed the receiver onto the cradle in her lap, made a most obscene gesture at it, crossed her arms belligerently, and hissed, "That's for you, sweetheart!"

Rick Lang smiled widely, carefully wiped the expression from his face, and quietly said, "Excuse me."

The chair whirled around so fast, her sunglasses slipped down her nose, and the receiver flew off its cradle. She caught it by the cord, set the whole thing on her desk, and came to her feet, blushing a deep crimson.

"How long have you been standing there?" she snapped.

"A while." He watched the color flood her face, her lips compress, and studied the oversized lenses that hid her eyes. "Sorry, I got here a little early." He smiled as he came forward, hand extended. "Rick Lang," he greeted simply.

"Allison Scott," she returned as his warm palm enfolded hers, pumped once, then disappeared into the pocket of a misshapen garment that had once been a letter jacket.

"You wanted to look me over." He stood back, absolutely at ease, weight on one foot, not so much as a hint of nervousness while that easy smile turned his mouth to magic and Allison had the distinct impression that if anyone was being looked over, it was she.

"Yes . . . I . . ." Her cheeks were positively hot. "Listen, I . . . I'm not a dishonest person." She gestured toward the phone, certain he'd seen her rude, unladylike gesture at the end of the conversation. "You heard me tell him I didn't really want to take scuba lessons, didn't you? I don't con people out of things, it's just that it's

kind of tough to come up with props for pictures sometimes, and I need scuba gear for a project I'm planning,
so I . . . I thought I just might give scuba diving a try if
it'd get me the gear and they'd let me have my money
back after lesson number one, but the guy got nasty and
I . . . I . . ." She suddenly realized she was blubbering to
hide her embarrassment, so fell silent. Being at a disad-
vantage was something new to Allison Scott, and letting
it show was even rarer.

Rick laughed engagingly, managing at the same time
to admire her upbeat look, the sleek jeans and body
sweater ending nearly at her knees, and her face, now
pink and flushed with embarrassment.

"I'm not here to judge you, you're here to judge me,
so forget I even heard it."

She told herself to cool down, that he was just another handsome face, another ego, another Jason. Yet
even at first glance she sensed a difference. The cocky
self-assurance was absent. Even his clothes were unsen-
sational. He was dressed as Mattie had warned he might
be—that seen-better-days jacket with the collar worn
absolutely threadbare; faded jeans; a pair of scuffed,
well-traveled almost-cowboy boots. The jacket was
partly unsnapped. Beneath it she saw a purple sweatshirt bearing a white number 12. Her eyes moved from
it to his face, which again affected her like a 110-volt
shock.

Ruddy skin, bitten to a becoming pink by the wind

outside, but smooth and unblemished; nose straight and shining from the cold. His hair had been styled by the feckless whims and guileless artistry of the January winds. That hair was, indeed, blond, a rich color that seemed a gift in the middle of this snowbound January, when most people bundled beneath warm caps. The lightly curled strands of hair were blown about his ears, temples, and forehead in engaging disarray. To comb it would be folly, she thought.

She suddenly realized she'd been staring, and looked away. He was, beyond a doubt, even better than his pictures.

"Did the agency tell you what this assignment is?" she asked.

"No, just that I should contact you to find out." He glanced across the studio—full gunnysacks resting against the front of an old, beaten desk; an ancient refrigerator; rolls of backdrop paper hanging from between the pipes on the ceiling; an assortment of chairs, stools, artificial plants, pillows, and cream cans in one corner; cameras on tripods, umbrella reflectors, strobes, a variety of photographic equipment. But mostly space—lots of space—and bright afternoon light flooding the place through the frost-laced windows. The corner where her desk stood was her "office," separated by two metal file cabinets against the wall, to one side. A nearby door led to a windowless room, but it was dark inside, and he couldn't tell what it was used for.

While he studied the studio, she studied him, wishing he were wearing a deep-necked shirt so she could see if there was hair on his chest. She wasn't quite sure how to ask him if there was. His eyes wandered back to hers, and she felt the color rise along her neck again.

"It's a book cover, and they need two poses, one for the front, one for the back."

"What kind of book?"

"A romance."

His eyebrows rose briefly, speculatively, then he shrugged and nodded.

"Have you ever posed with another model?"

"A few times."

"A woman?"

"Once."

"What was the ad for?"

"His and hers jogging suits or something like that."

She'd guessed right when studying the black-and-white glossy. He had the most utterly mobile mouth she'd ever seen and brows that expressed his mood almost before the words were out of his mouth.

"Will you do something for me?" Allison asked.

"If you'll do something for me." His eyes stopped roving and stared at his own reflection in her sunglasses. "Take off the glasses so I can see you."

"Oh!" She pushed the glasses up to rest on her hair. "I didn't realize."

"Better. Now where were we?"

"You were going to do something for me."

His hands came out of those drooping pockets, palms up. "Name it."

She moved from behind the desk to stand several feet before him, her hands slipped into the tight front pockets of her jeans, her shoulders hunched while she assessed him.

"Look angry," she ordered.

Again came the magic. In a split second his brows lowered, curling just enough to gain a viewer's sympathy yet not enough to make him look mean.

"Wily," she shot at him.

"What?"

"Look wily," she demanded, pointing a finger at his nose.

Immediately his gaze shifted until he peered from the corner of his eye at the refrigerator, as if it were there to thwart him but he had the goods on it.

Allison smiled, clapped her hands once in delight, then ordered, "Tired!"

His lips fell open slightly, a droop tugged the corners of his mouth down, and the sparkle disappeared from his spiky-lashed eyes, which he cast disconsolately at the floor between them. . . . Perfect, she thought.

Her heart went tripping over itself in delight. He was a natural! She went into a semi-crouch, hands grasping knees as if she were a lineman on a football team.

"Give me belligerent!" she threw at him.

The beautiful lips puckered up like a drawstring bag. The eyes scowled. The skin seemed to stretch tight over the sculptured cheekbones. She forgot his name, age, coloring, handsomeness, and saw only magic happening before her eyes. And while she was intensely captivated, caught up in discovering him, she didn't realize how her own eyes danced, how her face took on life, mirroring the responses he effortlessly brought forth with each new order she issued. No matter what it was, his face changed with each brusque command. "Threatened . . . amused . . . puzzled . . . pleased. . . ." As fast as she snapped out the words, he expressed them.

"Ardent!" she threw out.

For the first time his eyes settled on hers, remained on them, in full, while he leaned toward her as if only the merest thread of restraint compelled him not to touch. His eyes spoke poems, his lips hinted kisses, and his stance was so questing that she actually straightened and took a quick step backward.

Immediately he dropped the pose and took up his own lazy, loose-boned stance again, his eyes asking how he'd done.

The breath she expelled lifted wispy Pekingese bangs away from her forehead and temples, then she laughed, a bit nervously, but enormously pleased.

"Hey, do you do this all the time?" she asked.

"What?"

"This . . . this immediacy!"

He looked surprised. "Am I immediate?" He laughed a little.

"Immediate!" She became animated, pacing back and forth before him, boot heels clicking on the floor. "You're as immediate as electricity! Do you know what it sometimes takes to pull those kinds of responses out of models?"

"I never thought about it much. I haven't been in this racket very long. I just did what I was told."

"Yeah, you sure did." She came right up to him, smiling now, shaking her head in disbelief. Involuntarily, she took two steps backward.

Holy Moses! He didn't even know what he had. It was more than looks, more than bone structure and vibrant skin and come-hither eyes. It was . . . charisma! The kind photographers search for and rarely find. He quickly grasped each mood she sought to create and portrayed them not only with facial expression but with body language so poignant and natural that she hardly sensed him changing from one pose to the other until his mood caught her in the gut and telegraphed itself.

Suddenly realizing she was standing there clasping the top of her head as if trying to hold it on, she let her hands slide down and moved toward her desk, crossed her arms, and stared at the windows while stammering, "The . . . there's one other thing I have to ask you to do, and it may be rather unorthodox, but . . . I . . . I . . ."

He noted the defensive way she turned her back and

crossed her arms. "You haven't seen me running yet, have you? So what's next?" He smiled.

She glanced back over her shoulder. "Take off your jacket."

"It's off," he claimed, snaps flying open even as he spoke. He dropped the jacket nonchalantly across one corner of her desk.

His arms and chest filled out the jersey beautifully. She took a gulp and reminded herself he was just a model.

"Now the jersey."

That one slowed him down for a fraction of a minute.

"The jersey . . . sure." It came off, but a little slower than the jacket.

He was now in a white V-neck T-shirt, the jersey bunched up in one uncertain hand as if he were getting ready to pitch it at the first thing that threatened.

"The T-shirt, too," she ordered.

He illustrated "suspicious" without being ordered to. His magnificent eyes skittered to her, to the desk top, to the wall where a few totally unobjectionable samples of her work were displayed. Finally, frowning, his eyes came to rest on her. "Hey, lady—"

She spun to face him fully. "The name is Scott, Allison Scott."

"Okay, Ms. Scott, I don't do any of that kinky stuff that I've heard—"

"Neither do I, Mr. Lang!"

"Well, just what kind of book is this, anyway?"

"It's not pornography, if that's what you're thinking. But if you're scared to take off the shirt, I've got a file full of faces that'll suffice just as nicely as yours!"

"I guess I'd like to know why first."

"I told you, it's a romance. It takes place on Sanibel Island." Why was she being so defensive, she wondered. Because suddenly, when confronted with such an impressive physical specimen, she found she was wondering what he looked like bare-chested—and wondering out of mere female curiosity, not just artistic professionalism. Immediately she realized her mistake—it was amateurish and childish to be hedging the issue. She should have asked him immediately and avoided all mystery. Allison decided to be honest.

"All I need to know is if you have hair on your chest, but I felt a little silly asking."

Without another word the T-shirt came off. He stood before her in those tight, washed-out blue jeans, the nipples of his chest puckered up in the old icebox of a building, while zephyrs of too-fresh air sneaked along the floors. His was the first naked chest she'd seen since Jason departed, and Allison found she had to force her thoughts into structured paths while viewing it. But it was difficult to disassociate herself from the fact that he was—masculinely speaking—superb. Allison felt her body radiating enough heat to melt every shred of ice off those windows while he stood before her, shivering, letting her study him.

He looked down his chest, then back up at her. "Enough?" he asked.

For a moment she felt like a curious teenager peeping at the boys through a knothole in the changing-room wall, while he stood before her thoroughly at ease.

"Yes," she answered, and immediately the shirts started coming back over his head. From inside the first he asked, "So what am I going to wear for this picture?"

"Bathing trunks. Have you got any?"

"Sure." His head popped out, hair tousled in gamin boyishness that belied the mature, well-proportioned body she'd just assessed.

"What color are they?" she asked, moving back around the desk.

"White."

"Perfect, since we'll be shooting at night and they'll show up more."

His eyebrows curled and again he watched her warily as she moved, businesslike, to pick up pencil and clipboard, making a note while asking, "Do you have any scars on your legs or back?"

"No." He tossed the jersey on, shivering visibly now.

"Do you have any objections to kissing a stranger?"

With one arm half drawn into his jacket sleeve, he stopped, as if struck dumb.

"Kissing a stranger?"

"Yes." She raised serious eyes to his, making a desperate effort to appear calm.

"Who?"

Allison plucked the photo of the chosen female model from the pile on her desk and handed it to him. "Her."

He gave it a cursory glance. "The other subject in the photo, I take it?"

"Yes, if her coloring turns out to be right when I see her."

He turned it over and read the name on the back. "Vivien Zuchinski." He laughed and shook his head, lifting some of the tension from the room. "With a name like that she'd better know how to kiss!"

It broke the ice. Their eyes met and he chuckled first, followed by her mellow sounds of mirth.

"I feel like an ass," she admitted, relaxing even further, at last able to look him in the eye again.

"Well, I was a little uncomfortable there for a minute myself."

She ambled past the windows, toward the back of the studio, away from him. "I've never hired anybody for this kind of assignment before. I went about it all wrong. I apologize for making you feel ill at ease." She turned a brief glance back over her shoulder. He was still beside the desk.

"It's okay . . . as long as I get to kiss . . ." He checked the back of the photo again, "Vivien Zuchinski," he finished with a grin. He tossed the photo back onto the desk and followed Allison along the length of the studio.

"Do you mind my asking *you* a few things?" Rick Lang queried.

"No, ask away."

"Well, for starters, why are we shooting at night?"

She couldn't help smiling. "I can see you're still suspicious, Mr. Lang."

"Well, you have to admit it sounds a little fishy."

"Not when you want a nighttime effect. It's going to be a beach scene with a fire. I'll need total darkness outside so I can control the lighting. As you can see, the place is solid windows." She waved a hand at the glass wall and scanned the length of the studio before her eyes came to rest on him.

"A fire?" he repeated dubiously.

"Yup." With her hands in her pockets, one eyebrow raised slightly higher than the other, she looked a trifle smug.

"In here?" he asked skeptically.

"In here. You don't believe I can do it?"

He shrugged. "It'll be a good trick if you do. How many shots are you planning to take?"

"Oh, sixty-five maybe . . . of each cover, front and back."

He whistled softly. If she took that many shots, she was serious, dedicated, and thorough. He glanced around, obviously searching for a beach.

"Trust me," she said. "When you come for the ses-

sion there'll be a beach. And all you have to do is wear a
bathing suit and kiss a pretty girl. Is that so tough?"

"Not at all."

"Then do you want the job or not, Mr. Lang?"

"This is really on the level? Nothing kinky?"

"Honestly, you *are* a skeptic, aren't you? I admit the
poses will be sensual. There'll be body contact—after
all, it is a romance. But the final result will be tasteful."

A teasing light came into Rick's eyes. "Hmm . . . it's
beginning to sound like more fun all the time."

"Then you'll do it?"

"When do we shoot?"

"Thursday night, if things go right. I've got to create
the set first, and this one might give me a little trouble."

"The scuba gear?"

"No, not that. That's for the next series I'm doing. I
was just planning ahead. It's the beach that's going to
give me trouble on this one. I'll face the scuba gear
later."

"Would it help you out if I borrowed some from a
friend of mine?"

Her face registered pleased surprise. "Could you really?"

He glanced at the snowy city below. "I really don't
think he's putting it to very hard use right now, do you?"

"And I wouldn't have to take scuba lessons and get the
bends?" She feigned great relief, then added seriously,

"Taking the pictures is often the easiest part. It's setting them up that makes my hair turn gray sometimes."

"I hadn't noticed." He raised his eyes to the top of her head, then let them drift back to her face, an easy smile on his lips.

Immediately she was on her guard. It was the kind of remark Jason might have made, that sly, flattering brand of innuendo that had broken down her barriers and made her break her one basic rule of thumb: never get personal with the male models.

Though it was meant as banter, not flattery, the moment the words were out of Rick Lang's mouth he noticed how she crossed her arms tightly across her ribs. She was a classy-looking woman, particularly when she let her guard down. But often she set up unconscious barriers—the crossed arms, the lowered sunglasses, jumping behind the desk. He couldn't help but wonder what made her so defensive.

"I'll drop the gear by some afternoon."

"Oh, you don't have to do that. I can pick it up, wherever he lives."

"It's no trouble."

"I appreciate it, really. And thanks."

"Think nothing of it." He opened the door, turned with a grin, and finished, "As long as I get to kiss Vivien Zucchini."

"Zuchinski," she corrected, unable to stop the smile from spreading across her lips.

"Zuchinski."

Then he was gone.

Allison's arms slowly came uncrossed. She stared at the door, picturing his face, his form, his too-good-to-be-true physique. Unconsciously she slipped one hand through her long hair, kneading the back of her neck where pleasant tingles displaced common sense.

Haven't you learned your lesson yet, Scott? He's just another pretty boy out to make a score, and don't forget it!

Chapter
THREE

VIVIEN Zuchinski turned out to have exactly the right color and length of hair. Her face wasn't quite as long as her publicity photo made it appear, but she had flawless skin, still clinging to most of last summer's tan, and a mouth that could be called nothing but voluptuous. Her eyes were a stunning blue, as big as fifty-cent pieces, eyes, Allison knew, that would photograph beautifully, for they were fringed with sooty lashes so thick it seemed they'd weigh her down. Her breasts, it seemed, threatened to do the same. Oh, Vivien Zuchinski had all the qualifications, all right. Her main shortcoming, Allison could tell immediately, was that the girl was stupid, which—thankfully—would not show in a photograph. She chewed gum like an earth-breaking machine, had a fixation with lip gloss, which she constantly pulled out of her shoulder bag and painted on her pouting lips, whether in the midst of conversation or not. Her favorite word, which made Allison grimace, was "nice."

"Hey, *nice* studio," Vivien said immediately upon entering. "Hey, *nice* boots! Wheredja get them? I got a pair's kinda like them but not as nice. Those're really nice."

Allison cringed. Most of the models she worked with were intelligent, upbeat, many of them students on their way to professional careers in another field, helping themselves through college with the money they earned modeling. Vivien Zuchinski was definitely the exception to the rule.

"Hey, ah, what's the guy look like? Is he a fox, I mean, you know, ah, has he got a nice bod?"

"Very nice," Allison answered dryly. "Almost as nice as yours, Vivien."

"Hey, really? I like a guy with a nice bod."

It was all Allison could do to keep from rolling her eyes. "Have you got a bathing suit?"

"Oh, yeah, sure, got a bunch of 'em, nice ones, too."

"Would you mind bringing them along when you come?"

"Sure, you bet."

"The girl in the book wears a blue bikini."

"Hey, no sweat! I got this really nice blue bikini,

bought it last summer when this lifeguard up at Madden's kinda started givin' me the eye, you know? And I figure I'd just put on a little show for him and come out on the beach with a different bikini every day, but I only had five and I was gonna be there for six days, so, gol, what was I s'posed to do?" She flipped her palms up at shoulder height, hopelessly. "So I find this nice blue bik—"

"Vivien, bring them all, would you?"

Vivien was too much of a stereotype to be believable. She hung a hand on one hip, threw Allison a wide-eyed look of innocence, and answered, "Oh, sure . . . yeah, sure thing."

"Then I'll see you Thursday."

"Yeah, sure. Where'd you say you got them boots again?"

By the time Allison had gotten rid of Vivien she wondered if she'd made a mistake hiring her. Allison stood with hands on hips, shaking her head at the door through which Vivien had left, then glanced down at her own high-heeled boots and said to herself, "Nice boots, hey."

THE following afternoon Allison was standing disgruntledly with a broom and dustpan in her hand, spilled sand around her feet, when Rick Lang showed up with air tanks, flippers, hoses, and pipes.

"Hi."

She looked up, surprised, realizing in a flash how glad she was to see him again. "Oh, hi . . . oh, you brought them!" She dropped the dustpan, wiped her hands on her thighs, and came eagerly toward the door.

"Where do you want this stuff? It's kind of heavy."

She motioned toward the wall, sighed, and ran a hand through her hair. "Thanks. At least that's one thing that's gone right today."

"Have you got troubles?" He noted the sand, then her disgusted face. She noted his same old jeans and letter jacket, not at all the kind of clothing a guy wears to turn a girl's head.

"Have I ever." She glared at the mess. "I'm thinking about flying us down to Florida to do these shots! Except I think Vivien Zuchinski would drive me crazy before we got there."

"Vivien didn't turn out to be what you wanted?"

"Vivien's . . ." Allison searched for the proper word and turned a sardonic smirk his way. "Vivien's . . . *nice*."

He eyed the upward tilt of Allison's lips as she enjoyed some private joke. When she smiled, her eyes smiled with her mouth. She was dressed in off-white corduroy trousers with some kind of stylish, little army-green rubber shoes with bumpy white soles and long tongues and laces. They looked like something a socialite might wear duck hunting. Cute, he thought, taking in her modish hooded jacket and turtleneck sweater. Again she wore the sunglasses, pushed high up on her head.

"What's wrong with Vivien?"

"Nothing!" But there was a smirk of sarcasm in the quick word as she flipped her palms up innocently, then repeated, "Nothing. She has a terrific face and a very nice body."

"Good for me," he teased. "When can I kiss her?"

"Anytime you want . . . I'm sure she'll make that abundantly clear. You see, Miss Zuchinski has already pointed out the fact that she likes a guy with a, quote, 'nice bod,' unquote. Also, she likes her men foxy."

He laughed, leaning back, but it had a nice, easy sound, uncluttered by ego. "Need a hand?" he asked.

"I thought you'd never ask. The damn gunnysacks weigh a ton, and the first one came open halfway across the floor, which is not where I wanted to build my beach."

Already he was shucking off his frowsy letter jacket, laying it across the top of the refrigerator. "Just show me where."

She pointed to the area where the backdrop paper hung in huge rolls from the ceiling, then led the way, rolling aside some tall strobe lights on stands while he grabbed the ears of the closest gunnysack and dragged it over. She went to work cleaning up the loose sand while he moved the rest of the sacks. Covertly she watched the play of his back muscles as he lugged the bags.

"Do you go through this with every job you do?" He grunted, letting the first sack roll to its resting spot.

"Sometimes. I do what has to be done, get whatever props are necessary. You'd be surprised where trying to find them sometimes leads me."

"So I guessed when I walked in here the other day."

"A gentleman would tactfully refrain from mentioning the other day," she stated, her eyes on the broom while she swept. "Now the sand . . . I got it from a sand-and-gravel company, even got them to haul it up here free. In return I'll do a series of free shots of their operation when it's in full swing next summer. The kind of thing they can use on their Christmas calendar or whatever."

He glanced around the studio. "I never realized how much went into your kind of photography. In my kind the settings are already made for me."

"You're a photographer, too?" she asked, surprised.

"No, I'm a wildlife artist, but I paint from original photos."

She couldn't have been more surprised had he said he moonlighted as a fat man at the fair.

"An artist?" Yet the clothes fit, the lack of guile, of style.

"It's not a very lucrative business until you make a name for yourself. I only do the modeling to pay the bills."

"Like my school pictures."

"Your what?"

"I take school pictures . . . you know—little kids, stool, string-to-nose, smile and say *gravee-e-e!*" She made a clown face, tipping her head to one side, hands spread wide beside her ears, while the broom handle rested against her chest. "It pays the bills here, too."

"I thought that, working with publishers from New York, your career was going full swing."

"Not yet it isn't, but it will be," she stated, then set to work sweeping determinedly. "I had a good start once, but . . ." Suddenly her face closed over, and she bit off the remark abruptly. He waited, studying her as she again attacked her sweeping, this time too intensely.

"But what?" he couldn't resist asking.

"Nothing." Suddenly she dropped the broom and turned toward her files. "Hey, wanna see some of the things I've done for local ad agencies?"

"Sure, I'd love to," he answered agreeably, following her.

It took no more than thirty seconds of viewing her work for Rick Lang to see she had enormous talent. "You're good," he complimented, scarcely glancing up as he studied her work. "Your concepts are fresh and vital." It was true. Still objects seemed to have motion, moving objects to have speed, scented objects smell, and flavored objects taste. He noted that she had two favorite models—one male, one female—whom she'd used predominantly, as was the case with most commercial photographers.

"Thanks. I love the work, absolutely do."

"It shows." He glanced up, but she was staring at the top photo, one of the favorite male model. The man wore a textured shirt and was posed against a background of bleached barn boards and a rich, rough stone foundation. The ancient building created the perfect foil for the man's handsome face and classic clothing. This was no manufactured set. She'd taken the shot when the sun was low in the sky, either early morning or sunset, for the shadows, even on the rocks and boards, were dark, rich, and intense. Shot after shot showed an artist's soul, an enviable talent behind the viewfinder.

While Rick Lang leafed through the matted enlargements, Allison saw Jason's face flash past time and again. She felt a sense of loss as keenly as ever, this time a professional loss, for the works featuring him were the best of the lot. Oh yes, she'd lost much more than a lover when she'd lost Jason Ederlie.

Rick looked up and caught an expression of unconcealed pain on her features. Realizing he was studying her, a tinge of color stained Allison's cheeks before she quickly reached to flip through the pictures to one she particularly liked. "I sold this one to *Bon Appetit* magazine." It was a photo of freshly sliced apples and cheese viewed through a bottle of pale amber wine.

"Mmm . . . you make my mouth water," Rick said.

She shot him a censorious look, but he was only studying the photo. How often Jason had said things like that—glib, quick, thoughtless compliments, laced with his irresistible teasing grin, that were meant to do a snow job on her emotions while together they worked up an impressive portfolio of fashion shots of him alone. And, like a fool, she'd believed it all when he strung her along.

She swallowed now, trying to forget. Abruptly she lowered the sunglasses to cover her eyes, squared her shoulders, slipped her palms into her hip pockets, and walked away.

"Listen, thanks a lot for helping me haul the sand to where it belongs," she said. "I really appreciate it." The cool dismissal was unmistakable. It chilled the studio like air currents blowing across an icy tundra. Taken aback at her swift change, Rick's eyes narrowed, but he moved immediately toward his jacket.

"Sure. Anything else I can do before I leave?"

"No, I'm just about to close up here for the day."

"How about a cup of coffee? It's colder in here than it is outside."

"It always is, even though I crank up the radiators till they clank like a rhythm section. I'm used to it by now."

He waited, realizing she'd artfully glossed past his invitation without either accepting or rejecting it. "Maybe I'd better find one of those old-fashioned bathing suits, the ones shaped like long underwear, if it's always this cold in here."

"Oh, don't worry. Vivien will warm you up."

"You know, you've really got me wondering about this Vivien."

He managed to make Allison smile again, but her gaiety seemed to have seeped away. Her lips turned up, but this time the smile seemed forced.

"Oh, I never should have made any comment about Vivien. She's just a little . . . inane, that's all," Allison noted apologetically.

"Which is a polite way for saying she's not too bright."

"Who am I to say?" She hadn't been too bright herself, falling for Jason's line all those months. Maybe it was better to be like Vivien Zuchinski and look for a man with a nice body, have a good time with it for as long as you both were willing, and forget in-depth relationships.

Rick Lang had snapped up his old jacket, and stood now with his hands lost in its pockets.

"How come you hide behind those glasses like that all the time?"

"What? Oh . . . these!" She flipped them up with a false laugh. "I didn't even realize I had them on."

"I know."

Their eyes met, serious now, his gaze steady, blue, and determined. He stood between Allison and the door.

"A minute ago I asked you if you wanted to have a cup of coffee. I thought maybe you were hiding so you wouldn't have to answer."

She experienced a brief thrill before quelling it to wonder why he asked. Goodness, he was nice enough—Vivien's word, but apropos at the moment—and handsome enough to land any woman in the city. But no matter how inviting it sounded, Allison had learned her lesson.

"Thanks, but my work's not done for the day. I still have to find a log."

He shook his head slightly, as if to clear it. "A what? You lost me somewhere."

"A log. I need a log for the beach, and I've kept putting it off and putting it off because it's been so cold, and I have to go out in the woods somewhere—if I can find a woods—and haul a log in here."

He gestured across the room. "You couldn't haul those bags of sand across the floor, yet you're going to haul a log out of the woods, into your car—"

"It's a van."

"Into your van, up the freight elevator that works whenever it feels like it, down the hall, and in here, all by yourself?"

She shrugged. "I'm going to try."

"No, you're not. You'll slip a disc, and I'll never get to kiss Vivien Zucchini."

Without warning she spurted into laughter. "Zuchinski," she corrected, "and I'm not too sure it would be such a great loss if you missed the chance."

"Oh yeah? Let me be the judge of that. I'm helping you do the logging because Miss Zucchini sounds like something mighty delicious. Maybe I like women with nice bods, too, and foxy faces." But his eyes were filled with mischief. He stood there in those raunchy old boots and that shapeless old jacket, with his hair all messed, for all the world as ordinary as any plumber or grocer or accountant. And dammit! she liked him. Not just because he had a face fit for the silver screen, but because he managed to be persuasive without being pushy, had a swift sense of humor, and was the first man who'd invited Allison out for coffee in over a year—and that included Jason Ederlie, who'd only drunk hers and never even washed his cup!

"Maybe we could pick up a cup of coffee and take it with us in the van," she suggested, then admitted, "I *am* freezing, and we're running out of daylight if we expect to come up with a log."

He smiled—not big, not phony, not even at her—and gestured with a shoulder. "Let's go." From the coat tree behind the door she grabbed her jacket, but he plucked it from her hands and helped her put it on. It was something Jason had never done. Thinking back on it, in that passing instant, Allison realized there were actually times when *she'd* held *his* sport coat while he slipped flawless shirtsleeves into it. Often, afterward, she hugged him from behind, using the jacket for an excuse to touch, to caress.

She'd forgotten how it felt to have a man help her into a coat. It made her more conscious than ever of Rick Lang as they rode down in the clanking old freight elevator together. She stared at the brass expansion gate, then at the ancient floor indicator, ill at ease as she sensed him studying her.

When they reached her van, he surprised her by following her to the driver's side, taking the keys from her gloved hand, removing his own gloves and unlocking the door. She found herself staring in disbelief. Did men actually do these things anymore?

He smiled, handed her the keys, waited for her to climb in so he could slam the door, then jogged around to the other side. He climbed in, hunched up, and chafed his arms.

"Not many guys do that anymore," she noted.

"Do what?"

"Help with coats and car doors and things."

"My mother used to cuff me on the side of the head if I forgot. After about the twenty-ninth cuff, I managed to remember. After that it kind of stuck with me. Guess I still think she'll manage to get me if I forget."

She couldn't help laughing. The story made him seem infinitely more human.

"God, but it's cold." He shivered, then pointed out the windshield and peered through the frosty glass as the engine chugged to life. "Go south and take Highway 12. I'll show you a place right in the middle of the city limits where we can get you your log."

"In the middle of the city?"

"Well, almost. Theodore Wirth Park."

"Theodore Wirth! But it's public land! It's against the law. If they catch us, we'll get fined."

He grinned, all lopsided and little-boyish. "Guess my mother didn't cuff me quite enough. Sounds like fun, trying to put one over on the law. Course, it's up to you . . . I mean, I don't want to be the one responsible for getting your name on the FBI's Ten Most Wanted List."

She laughed again. "You do that, and I'll personally see to it you never kiss Vivien Zucchini."

"Zuchinski," he returned with a smile coming from deep inside his turned-up collar and hunched-up shoulders. "And you'll have a tough time of it from behind the walls of the state pen."

They were thoroughly enjoying each other as the van headed toward Theodore Wirth Park. Allison stopped at a sandwich shop and Rick jumped out, returning a few minutes later with cups of hot coffee. The late-afternoon sun lit the clouds around it into crazy zigzags of aqua blue and vibrant pink. But suddenly Allison didn't mind the frigid temperatures.

Rick handed her a cup of coffee, watching appreciatively while she caught the fingers of her gloves between her teeth and yanked them off. He grinned broadly at the sight of her in the worst-looking bobcap he'd ever seen, pulled so low that her eyebrows scarcely showed.

"Forgot to ask if you like cream or sugar," he said.

"Sugar, usually, but I'd drink it any way today."

"Sorry. I'll remember next time." He sipped, looking around. "Nice van."

"Yup, it is, isn't it? Only another year and a half and it'll be paid for. I need it. I'm always hauling junk back and forth from the studio. Buying a van was the smartest move I ever made."

"I'm not big on vehicles," he offered. "Don't really care if I have a tin lizzy or an XKE—as long as it'll get me there, that's all that matters."

It had always been Jason's dream to have a sleek, silver Porsche, one that would set off his looks with a touch of panache. How refreshing to find a man whose values were so different.

"Would you look at that sky," Rick Lang said admiringly, almost as if reading her mind.

"Beautiful, huh?" They fell into comfortable silence, driving westward, squinting into the lowering sun against which every object became bold, black, and striking. Even the telephone lines, power poles, and road signs became artistic creations when viewed against the brilliant sky.

How long had it been since she had enjoyed a ride

through an icy, stinging wintry afternoon and not complained about the cold? Allison wondered. Now she found herself noting the silhouettes of oaks standing blackly against their backdrop as she turned the van onto Wirth Parkway and entered the sprawling, woodsy park.

Children were sliding down the enormous hills between sections of wooded land. Skiers were out on the runs in gaily colored clothing. Even a sweatsuited jogger could be seen, his breath labored and hanging frozen in the air.

The road wove into the heart of the public land, past frozen Wirth Lake, the ski chalet, the ski jump, and acres of untouched woodland, which surprised and delighted Allison, situated as it was in the center of the teeming city. The van moved in and out of shadows as the late sun rested lower and lower in the west, behind the trees, making long, skinny shadow fingers across the road.

Rick directed Allison up a steep incline at a sign that read Eloise Butler Wildflower Garden and Bird Sanctuary.

"Anybody who's looking for wildflowers today is going to be disappointed," he commented. "I think we can steal our log up there without getting caught."

At the top was a paved parking lot the plows hadn't bothered to clear. Tracks left by cross-country skiers showed that only they had disturbed the snow here.

"You gonna be warm enough?" Allison asked as Rick opened his door.

"Yup!" He produced warm leather gloves from his pocket, yanked his collar higher for good measure, and got out.

It was getting dark quickly as they entered the woods, following the foot trails whose wooden identification signs now wore caps of snow. The trails were easy to follow, and when Allison and Rick were scarcely twenty-five feet from the van, they spotted a long, oblique lump beneath a thick coat of snow. Rick brushed it off, revealing a four-foot section of tree trunk.

"How's this?" he asked, squatting beside it and looking up.

She glanced measuringly from the log to the van. "Close, but too heavy, I think."

He walked to the end, kicked around in the snow, knelt, and boosted it up from the ground. "Must be half-rotten, just the kind we need so we can run fast when the posse comes."

"Think I can lift it?" she asked.

"I don't know. Give it a try."

She shuffled through the snow to the other end of the log, rummaged around to find a handhold, grunted exaggeratedly, and hoisted up her end. "I did it! I did it!" She staggered a little for good measure.

Rick trained his eyes on a spot behind her shoulder and said with grave seriousness, "Oh, officer, it wasn't me! I was just coming to turn in this lady for stealing this rotten log. Ninety-nine years should certainly be fair, yes, whatever you say."

Allison gave a giant shove, and the log rammed Rick Lang in his beautifully muscled belly like a battering ram, then thudded to the earth at his feet as he dramatically clutched his gut. He staggered around as if he'd just had his lights punched out, hugged himself, and grunted, "I . . . I take that back . . . off . . . officer, let her go. I'll pay for the damn log!"

She affected a wholly superior air and joined his farce. "Officer, all this man's done all day long is talk about kissing girls. Can you blame a woman for grabbing the first thing in sight to protect herself with?"

Rick raised both gloved hands as if a gun were pointed at his chest. "Oh no . . . oh no, no, no, I'm innocent. Furthermore, after this display, you can put your damn log in your van by yourself! I'm going for a walk!"

He turned and continued along the trail, leaving her standing up to her knees in snow, laughing.

"Hey, no fair, you've got high boots and my shoes only go up to my ankles. . . ." She paused to check for sure, lifting one foot. She raised her voice and called after him, "Not even that high!"

"Come on. I'll make tracks," he said without pausing, dragging his feet to plow a way for her. It was somewhat better, but certainly left plenty of snow for her to trudge through. With high, running steps she hurried to catch up with him.

"Hey, wait up, you crazy man!" she hollered.

He paused, only half-turned to watch her over his shoulder. When she was close behind, he headed again along the footpath, with her at his heels.

It had been years and years since Allison had been in the woods at this time of day. The sky turned lavender as the sun sank. Snow blanketed everything, muffling sound, softening edges, warming—in its own way—all that lay around them.

Suddenly Rick stopped short and stood with his back to her, stalk still. Automatically she stopped, too. Sparrows tittered from branches above their heads, the notes crisp in the clear air. Wordlessly, Rick pointed. Allison's eyes followed. There on the snow beneath a giant tree sat a brilliant red cardinal.

"That's the kind of stuff I photograph and paint," he whispered.

The cardinal flitted away at the sound of his voice. Allison watched it flash through the trees. Suddenly she felt curiously refreshed and renewed. She turned in a circle, gazing at the white-rimmed branches overhead. "It's hard to believe we're in the heart of the city."

"Haven't you ever been here before?" He still faced away from her, and she looked up at blond hair curling over his upturned collar, then scanned the peaceful woods again.

"No. Not up here. I've been through the park, but I never bothered to come up here and see what was at the end of the trail."

He stood in silence, studying the sky, his head tipped sharply back. After a long time he said, "It's peaceful, isn't it?"

"Mmm-hmm." Even the birds had stopped twittering. She realized she could actually hear Rick Lang's breathing. They fell silent again, two people whose busy lives afforded too little of such elemental joys as this. There came a faint popping, as if bark were stretching in its sleep, growing restless for spring.

"This is what I miss about not living where I was born and raised."

"Are you a country boy?"

"Yup." Suddenly he seemed to grow aware of how long they'd been standing motionless, knee-deep in snow. "Your feet must be frozen."

"It's worth it," she replied, and found it true.

"Better get you back though, and steal that log if we're going to."

"I guess." Still, she was reluctant to return to the highway, to the sound of cars that was totally absent here, to the road signs instead of boles and branches.

"Can you even feel your feet anymore?"

Grinning, she looked down, then back up at him. His face was almost obscured by oncoming dark. "What feet?"

He laughed. "Just a minute, stay where you are," he ordered, then jogged off the path, circled around her, hunched over, and said, "Climb on."

"What!"

"Climb on." His butt pointed her way. "I got you into this mess, I'll get you out."

"Won't do you a bit of good. They're gone. The feet are gone. Can't feel a thing down there," she said woefully, staring at her hidden calves.

"Get the hell on, you're making me feel guiltier by the minute."

"Oh, lord, if I do, you'll be the one with the slipped disc."

"From a willow whip like you? Don't make me laugh."

So she clambered aboard Rick Lang's back, and he clamped a strong arm around each leg. She found herself with her cheek pressed against the back of his jacket, gloved hands clasped around his neck as she rode piggyback to the parking lot. Childish, foolish . . . fun, she thought.

He smelled of cold air and slightly of something scented, like soap or shaving lotion. Bumping along, she tried to think back to how she had managed to end up in such a spot. She could scarcely remember. Only that it had been painless, fun, and that somehow he'd managed to make her laugh again.

At the van she slipped off him and they loaded the log without mishap, but by that time Allison was shivering like a wet pup.

"Do you want me to drive back?" Rick asked. "You could stick your feet up underneath the heater and start thawing out."

"No, they're too cold. If I thaw them out that fast I'll lose 'em for sure."

"Minnesota girls!" he exclaimed in disgust. "Never know how to dress for the weather, even though they're born and raised in it."

"How do you know I was born and raised in it?"

"Were you?"

"Nope, South Dakota."

"Hey, you wanna talk all night or get back to town so you can thaw out?"

When they were halfway back to the city, the headlights picking the way through the dark, she asked, "Are you always this way?"

"What way?"

She shrugged. "I don't know . . . amusing."

She felt his eyes scan her for a moment before he turned away and answered, "When I'm happy."

Memories of Jason came flooding back, warning her again of how sweet words such as these had hurt her once before, led her into a trap that had been sprung with such suddenness that she hadn't yet healed. This man was too new, too irresistible, too perfect. She was reacting to the loss of Jason, spinning Rick into a fanciful hero of her liking.

They parked the van on the nearly deserted downtown street and unloaded the log. Carrying it down the hall of the Genesis Building, they met the night watchman. As congenially and off the cuff as if the enormous log were only a toothpick he'd been picking his teeth with, Rick nodded to the curious old man, asked, "Hey, how's it going?" and marched on past without so much as a snicker.

After they'd gotten into the ancient elevator and propped the ungainly log in the corner, between them, they turned around to see the gates closing on the night watchman's suspicious face.

Allison and Rick looked at each other and crumpled against the sides of the elevator in laughter.

"He's probably still standing there with his tonsils showing," she managed at last.

"This is probably the most intrigue he's had since he got the job. We'll keep him wondering for months what we did with a log this size on the sixth floor of a downtown office building."

They were still in stitches as they lugged the clunky log down the hall and into the studio, stumbling under its weight, which was far more appreciable the farther they went. When they'd deposited it inside, near the sandbags, Rick dropped down heavily on it, puffing.

"When I took this modeling job, I had no idea what else it would entail."

"Listen . . . thanks. I realize now I'd never have been able to do it alone."

"Any time."

The room grew quiet. Somewhere in the hall the elevator reverberated as it moved in the silent building.

"Probably the night watchman coming up to see what those two crazy people are up to," suggested Rick.

"I'll explain to him someday."

Rick clamped his hands to his knees and lunged to his feet.

"Well, I've got an appointment on a log with Vivien Zucchini Thursday night. I'd better get home and get my beauty rest."

Allison led the way to the door, switched out the lights, locked up, and walked with Rick to the elevator. The night watchman was standing there again, studying them with a curious look on his face.

As the cage was cutting him off from view, Rick waved two fingers at him. "G'night."

Unable to resist, Allison did the same.

"He has the master key. How much you wanna bet he goes into the studio and figures it all out?"

There seemed little more to say. Allison felt a strange reluctance to leave Rick. He walked her to the van and opened her door again.

"Well, thanks for the ride," he said.

"Same to you." She smiled.

He grinned, slammed the door, gave a good-bye salute, and sent Allison on her way wondering again where his hidden flaw was. Surely it would show up soon. The man was too good to be true.

Chapter
FOUR

T HE following day Allison had an argument with a stubborn fool at the Anderson Lumberyard who refused to deliver a partial pallet of bricks because its value was under fifty dollars. When she explained her situation, he became even more belligerent, his raspy voice taking on an insolent tone. "Lady, we don't deliver bricks to no sixth floor of no office building. If we can't unload 'em with a forklift, we don't unload 'em at all. You want your bricks up there, you carry 'em up yourself!"

"But—"

The dead wire told her she was talking to nobody. She slammed the receiver down and kicked the corner of her desk, angered as she so often was by things beyond her control.

The phone rang and without thinking she jerked it to her ear and bawled into the mouthpiece, "Yaa, hullo!"

A few seconds of surprised silence passed, then a man's voice said, "Oh, I must have the wrong number."

Realizing how rudely she'd answered, she clutched the phone and put on a far more congenial voice. "No . . . wait, sorry, this is Photo Images. What can I do for you?"

"Ms. Scott?"

"Yes, who . . . oh God, is this Rick Lang?"

"You guessed it. Caught you being nasty on the phone again."

She sank into her swivel chair and hooked her boot heels on the edge of the desk. "Listen, I'm sorry. You must think I'm a real asp, but sometimes I get so mad at . . . at . . . well, at men!"

"Hey, what'd I do?"

"Oh, it's not you, but do you mind if I blow off a little steam? I mean, all I asked for was a little partial load of bricks, and you'd think that damn fool could tell his truck driver to pull his truck up in front of the building and deposit them on the sidewalk or something! I mean, I wasn't asking to have them hand carried up six flights!

But no, the load isn't worth enough for them to waste the gas. If they can't take it off with a forklift, they won't take it off at all!"

From his end Lang heard an ending sound like the growl of an angry bear while she worked off her frustration.

At her end, Allison felt slightly sheepish when his understanding laugh came over the wire and he asked good-naturedly, "There, do you feel better now?"

"No, dammit, I'll have to carry those bricks by myself . . . yes, kind of . . . oh hell, I don't know!" she blurted out in exasperation. But a minute later, Allison found her anger losing steam and finally disintegrating into self-effacing laughter. "Hey, I'm really sorry I took it out on you. It's not your fault. And what if you'd been a paying customer wanting to hire me? I'd have alienated you with the first word."

"How do you know you didn't? You still don't know what I called for."

Allison dropped her feet to the floor, crossed her legs, leaned an elbow on the desk, and affected a sultry, ingratiating feminine drawl. "Good mawnin' dahlin', this's Photo Images—hot coffee, hugs of greetin', and free makeup with every sittin', honey, so y'all come back, heah?"

She was twisting a strand of hair coyly around an index finger as Lang's full-throated laughter came over the wire, and she pictured him as he'd been last night in the woods, goofing around with the log, giving her a piggy-back ride.

But now he reminded Allison, "Hey, I didn't get any hugs of greeting, and if I remember right, I'm the one who bought the coffee."

"But you'll get free makeup when I take the shots, and I'll buy you a cup of coffee then, so we'll be even."

"What about the hug?"

Something fluttery and warm lifted Allison's heart. She knew she was engaging in mild flirtation and shouldn't be. She searched for a glib answer, leaning back and gazing at the ceiling. "Mmm, what about when you gave me that piggyback ride? What would you call that?"

"You're too quick, Ms. Allison Scott. I'll let you off this time. What I called for was to check on your health today after last night's frostbite in those flimsy little duck shoes of yours."

"No worse for wear."

"Not even a head cold?"

"Not even."

"Well, good, at least I didn't add another item to your list of grievances against . . . men."

Allison smiled, toying now with the dial on the phone, warmed by his thoughtfulness, though she didn't want to be. But it had been a long time since anyone other than Mattie had been concerned about her welfare.

Certainly Jason had never been. With Jason it was always her catering to him.

"Listen, what's all this about the bricks anyway? Can I help?" he offered.

"No, it's not your problem, it's mine. I need them to weigh down the plastic so I can build a lake."

"You're kidding!"

"No, I'm not! Have you ever heard of a beach without a lake?"

"Wouldn't it have been easier to take the pictures in the summer and use a real lake?"

"No challenge in that."

"Oh, you like a challenge, do you, Ms. Scott?"

"Rather. Besides, contracts like this don't always accommodate the seasons. I knew when I accepted that it would present problems, but it was just too good a chance to pass up. This cover will be for a new line of books coming out next year, and if I give them what they want, chances are I'll have my foot in the door. It'd be wonderful to know where my next month's grocery money was coming from . . . and the next, and the next."

"I know the feeling well and I admire your guts, but I'll still have to see it to believe it—a lake, a beach, and a bonfire?"

"Do you doubt me, Mr. Lang?"

"I have the feeling I shouldn't, but I do. It sounds impossible."

"Nothing is impossible if you want it badly enough, and I want this to be the best damn cover Hathaway Romances sees between now and June, so they beat my door down to get me to do a hundred more."

Rick Lang was beginning to admire the lady more and more. He couldn't wait to see how in the world she would build that lake. "So what about the bricks? Could I help? I haven't got a forklift, but I've got two good hands."

"Listen, you've done enough already, helping me get that log up here. I can handle the rest myself. The only thing is, if it takes me longer than I thought, we might have to delay the shooting for a day. But I'll call you and let you know when the set is ready. If we can't shoot Thursday, could you make it Friday instead?"

"Sure . . . whenever."

There was a pause in the conversation, and Allison suddenly felt reluctant to end it. Rick Lang was turning out to be one of the most congenial and warm men she'd ever met.

"Well . . . thank you again for checking on me, but as I said, there's no need to start cooking chicken soup."

"My pet hen will be glad to hear that."

They laughed together for a moment, and the line seemed to hum with expectancy.

"I'll call," Allison promised. "See you either Thursday or Friday night, six o'clock."

"Right. Bye."

But after the word was spoken Allison waited for a click, telling her Rick Lang had hung up. A full ten seconds passed, and she heard nothing. A curious throat-filling exhilaration tightened her skin, like back in high school when the boy you had a crush on stared at you across the classroom for the first time. Five more seconds of silence hummed past, and at last Allison heard the click. As if the phone had turned hot, she dropped the receiver onto the cradle, jumped back, and jammed her hands hard into her pants pockets, staring at the instrument with her heart hammering in her temples.

Scott, you're a giddy fool! she harped silently. Go get your load of bricks!

She drove the van to the lumber yard, where she bought a roll of strong, black plastic and the partial pallet of bricks. When she started loading them single-handedly, the men at the loading dock felt sheepish enough to lend a hand.

Back at the Genesis Building it took almost two hours to round up the head janitor and locate a freight dolly, and by that time Allison's temper was flaring again. At this rate she might as well wait and shoot the scenes at Lake Calhoun, come summer!

By four o'clock in the afternoon it was cold and windy in the canyons between the tall buildings as she backed the van up to the dock platform. The alley was dismal, foreboding, and the cold was no palliative for her temper. Allison shivered, then pulled on leather gloves and began the arduous task of transferring the bricks two at a time from the van to the wide, flat dolly. According to the radio, the windchill had sent the temperature down to minus forty. Allison tugged the thick knit cap lower over her ears and forehead. The icy air caused a pain smack between her eyes. As she bent and stooped, the wind seemed to swirl and chill and find every hidden path into the breaks between her layers of clothing.

Damn that stingy lumberyard! she cursed silently, thunking down two bricks and turning back for two more. Allison's nose was drippy, and her fingers had turned to icicles. She looked like a disgruntled kodiak bear, bundled up in an ugly old army-green parka with her hat covering her eyebrows.

"Ms. Scott, you're going to give yourself a hernia if you don't slow down."

Allison spun around, a brick in each hand, and peered from the depths of the van to find Rick Lang lounging against the doorway beside the freight dolly, smiling in amusement. The ugly, utilitarian bobcap had slipped so far down it now almost covered her eyes. She had to tip her head way back to peer at him from under it. At that moment, to Allison's horror, she felt a trickle of mucous run warmly from her nose down to her lip. Sniffing frantically, she thought, Oh no! Oh dear! I look like the abominable snowman! And damn, why did my nose have to run right now?

"Oh, God, how did you find me here?" she wailed.

"The studio was unlocked and the lights were on, so I figured you must be unloading bricks—I thought you'd be at the loading dock."

Before she could hide or run, he was pulling on thick leather gloves and bounding onto the back of the van. Automatically she bent over and covered her head with both hands. From the muffled depths came the wail, "Ohhhhhhh, hell! I look like the wrath of God."

He answered with a wide-mouthed laugh, then she felt a hand rough up her bobcap teasingly and push her face momentarily farther toward her knees.

"Hey, you look like an honest working woman, so let's get to work."

When spring comes, she promised herself, I'm gonna bury this ugly cap in the garden!

She stood up, knowing her face was beet red, thankful he couldn't see much of it in the dim light of the dock area. She peered up into his smiling blue eyes, sliding the bobcap farther back on her head. Immediately it slid back where it wanted to be, and any lingering delusions Allison might have had about her appearance vanished. She must be about as appealing as a seven-year-old boy after an afternoon of sledding.

Horrified, she felt her nose dripping again. Rick Lang just stood there and boldly laughed at her, a pair of bricks in his hands.

"Hey, your nose is dripping," he informed her merrily.

She sniffed loudly, leaned farther back, purposely exaggerating her snot-nosed, childish appearance, swiped at her nose with the back of her gloved hand and pouted, "Well, I don't have a tissue, smarty! And if you were any kind of a gentleman whatsoever, you would politely refrain from mentioning it!"

He chuckled and dropped one brick. "It's rather hard to pretend when it's running right down." Leaning sideways, he fished in a hind pocket and came up with a crumpled white hanky. "It looks like it's been used, but it hasn't," he informed Allison. "I do my own laundry and ironing isn't really one of my favorite pastimes."

"Beggars can't be choosers," she returned, yanking off a glove and turning her back while she buried her nose in his hanky and honked. To the best of her knowledge it was the first time she'd ever used a man's hanky.

"How come in the movies when this happens to girls they are somehow always daintily indisposed, with clinging tendrils of hair coming seductively loose from their topknot?" she grumbled.

"I think I see one now." Behind her she felt a tug as

he lightly pulled a frowsy chunk of hair that must have been hanging from beneath her cap.

Never in her life had Allison felt more like an unfeminine klutz!

Rick Lang didn't mind one bit. He thought she looked delightful, bundled up in that ugly war-surplus parka, red nose running, scarcely an eyelash visible underneath that unflattering bobcap. She finished blowing her nose, turned, offered him the hanky, realized her mistake, and withdrew it with a snap. "Oh, I'll wash it first."

He unceremoniously yanked it out of her hand and buried it in his pocket. "Don't be silly. Let's load bricks."

He set to work with a refreshing vigor, unlike what she might have expected from a man with a cushy job like modeling. Somehow, when she'd first laid eyes on his snapshot, she'd visualized a self-pampering hedonist, but she was learning he was no such thing.

They had little breath for talking while they transferred the bricks from van to dolly. Their breath formed white puffs in the air as they worked. When they were finished, he ordered, "Toss me the keys. I'll pull the van in the lot, but wait for me. We'll take that dolly up together. Don't try to push it yourself."

He disappeared around the front of the van, and Allison lowered the big overhead door, evaluating Rick

Lang anew. It was wonderful to have a man offering to help with the heavy work. She had done it alone for so many years, she never thought much about it anymore. But a warm glow spread through her at his admonition to wait for him.

He came back in, handed her the keys, and took up his place at the far end of the dolly, gesturing toward the other end. "You steer, I'll push."

"Aye, aye, sir," she replied with a grin.

The dolly filled almost the entire area of the freight elevator. When they'd eased it on, Rick sat down on top of the bricks and indicated a place beside him. "Your chariot awaits," he quipped.

Allison laughed and plopped herself down beside him, Indian fashion, for the ride up to the sixth floor. From the corner of her eye she saw him turn his gaze from the floor indicator to her. Self-consciously she realized she was wearing the most ridiculously ugly pac boots ever manufactured. Resolutely she kept her head tilted back, eyes trained on the numbers above the door.

"That's a damn nice cap," he teased.

Without taking her eyes off the numbers, she pulled the disreputable hat even farther down over her forehead, until only a slit of eyes remained visible beneath the turned-back brim.

"For a stupid South Dakota girl who doesn't know

how to dress for the weather, it ain't too bad." She flashed him a smart smirk and a brief glimpse of the corner of one eye as it angled his way.

"I'll take that back when I see a beach, a lake, and a bonfire on the sixth floor."

"Doubting Thomas," she scoffed, and grinned.

They arrived at the sixth floor, and she leaped off the dolly and opened the clanking brass gate, then together they worked the ungainly vehicle into the hall. Wouldn't you know, the night watchman had just come on duty. He rounded a corner of the hall and saw the two of them maneuvering a load of bricks off the elevator.

Rick raised a hand in greeting and informed the wide-eyed fellow, "Just takin' my girl for a ride is all." He swept a theatrical bow toward the bricks, and Allison played along, clambering on board to again sit Indian fashion in snow boots, parka, and bobcap, while Rick pushed her down the hall to the studio door.

When they got inside they closed the door, looked at each other, and burst into laughter, as it seemed they were doing with increasing regularity. Rick dropped down onto the dolly. Allison leaned against the door, holding her sides, filled with rich amusement such as she hadn't shared with anyone in years.

"Oh, you were so glib, I think he believed you!" she managed to get out, quite weak now, reaching a

tired hand to doff the cap from her head, leaving behind a mop of hair as disheveled as a serving of
spaghetti.

"So were you—climbing on, sitting there like some
Indian princess on her way to a fertility rite. You were
superb!"

"I was, wasn't I?" she preened.

Immediately he reconsidered, scanning her from
head to foot. He shook his head in mock despair. "I
think I take that back. You're the biggest mess I've ever
seen in my life."

"How would you like a brick implanted in the middle
of your forehead?" She picked one up and threatened
him with it.

"Hey, come on." He raised his arms protectively
above his head. "Take a look in the mirror."

"*You* take a look in the mirror! Your hair looks like
somebody styled it with a cattle prod, so don't point fingers at me." She deposited the brick and turned toward
the doorway, across the room. Rick saw a light come on
as she moved inside, and the next minute he heard a
blood-curdling shriek.

He got up off the dolly and ambled over to the doorway, where he stood smiling. The well-lit room was apparently a dressing room, and Allison stood in front of a
mirror, sticking her tongue out at herself.

"See? I told you," he nettled.

"Yep," she agreed dryly. She found a comb in a nearby drawer and dragged it unceremoniously through her hair.

He stood watching, noting the way the winter air had tinted her nose a becoming pink, the way her feminine shape was lost inside the enormous parka, which now hung unzipped, dwarfing her shoulders.

At that moment a furious pounding sounded on the studio door, followed by the concerned voice of the night watchman. "Hey, you all right in there, miss?"

Allison's and Rick's eyes met in the mirror, and they giggled.

"The night watchman. Thinks you're being assaulted in here."

"You'd better stop making fun of my appearance or I'll tell him it's true." She gave him a warning glance.

"Hello in there!" came another shout from the hall.

Allison hotfooted it around Rick Lang, opened the hall door, and confronted the frowning, grandfatherly man who peered past her to the pallet of bricks, the log at the far end of the room, and Rick lounging against the doorway of the dressing room. "Everything all right in here?" he asked. "Thought I heard somebody screamin'."

"Oh, that was me." She pointed over her shoulder. "He tried to get fresh, but I've got a black belt in karate. **Thanks for inquiring, but I can take care of myself.**"

The watchman turned away, shaking his head and muttering to himself.

In the studio, Rick threatened, "If he sics the law on me, I'll tell 'em about the log you stole from a public park."

"I didn't steal that log, *you* did!"

"Oh yeah? Then what's it doing in your studio?"

She shrugged innocently. "Don't know. It just showed up here uninvited, like you."

Rick lazily pulled his shoulder away from the door frame, pulling on his gloves while he sauntered to the dolly and ordered, "Get your butt over here and help me unload these bricks, lady, before I take offense and leave you to do it yourself."

They worked companionably for the next two hours, placing the bricks in two roughly concentric circles on the floor at the far end of the studio. While Rick returned the dolly to the loading area, Allison unrolled the black plastic and sliced off an enormous piece to act as their lake bottom. When Rick came back, the two of them arranged the plastic, draping it over the inner circle of bricks, then weighing it with the outer circle. They crawled back and forth on their hands and knees in their stocking feet so they would not puncture the plastic, taking up slack, gauging how big the makeshift puddle of water had to be to produce an adequate reflection from the fill light that would simulate the moon shimmering upon the lake.

Next they worked with the sand. Allison was grateful to have Rick there to lug the clumsy sacks around the edge of the "lake." As they emptied them one by one, covering the brickwork, the setting slowly took shape, appearing less and less artificial. The last item to be positioned was the log. Together they hefted it, placed it in the foreground where Allison indicated, then stood back while she formed a square with her palms to confine the view the camera would see and to judge the results of their labor. She hadn't yet set up a camera on the tripod, but she asked Rick, "Will you sit on the log for a minute so I can get a general idea of how we did?"

"That's what I'm being paid for." Obligingly he sat on the log, his arms draped loosely over his knees while she studied the composition as best she could without everything in it.

He watched her kneel, her face serious now as she peered at him from about hip level, where the camera would be come Thursday night. Again she was all brisk self-assurance, a studious expression on her face as she did what she loved doing best. She had removed the army parka a while ago and now wore a white sweatshirt and blue jeans. As she bent forward, her hair fell across her cheek, but she seemed totally unaware of it, of anything but her work.

Suddenly she stood up, biting her upper lip while deep in thought. She glanced at the darkened strobes standing around the edges of the room, thought for a moment longer, abruptly smiled, clapped her hands, and declared, "Yup! It'll work just fine."

"Good," he returned, then sighed. He looked at his watch and reminded her, "Do you know what time it is? It's eight-thirty, and I haven't had any supper. Neither have you." He heaved himself to his feet, gestured with a sideward quirk of the head as he passed her, and led the way to the front door. "Come on, let me buy you a hamburger."

Walking toward their jackets piled on her desk, she scolded, "Oh no, not after all the help you've given me. It's me who'll do the buying."

He automatically picked up her parka first and held it, waiting for her arms to slip in. "I asked first."

"I buy or I'm not going," she declared stubbornly. "It's the least I can do."

"Are you always this obstinate?"

"Nope. Only when guys come along and save my discs."

"All right, you win." He shook the jacket slightly. "Come on, get in, I'm starved."

At last she complied, buttoning up, retrieving her bobcap, and pulling it clownishly low over her forehead again while he slid his arms into his jacket and snapped it up.

"My car or yours?" he asked as they walked toward the elevator.

"How 'bout both of ours, then we can just hit home after we eat."

"Right."

On the first floor he turned toward the front of the building, she toward the rear, having agreed upon where to meet. But when Allison got to her van she realized, chagrined, that she was almost flat out of cash. She counted the money in her billfold and her loose change. She had a single one-dollar bill and hardly enough change to make up the price of two hamburgers, much less drinks to go with them.

God, how embarrassing, she thought, and frantically started the van, thinking of her checkbook at home on the kitchen cabinet. The city streets were almost deserted. She had no idea what Rick's car looked like, so she had no recourse but to drive to the appointed restaurant and wait in the parking lot for him to arrive.

When she saw his face behind the window of a Ford sedan, she jumped from the van, left it idling, and was waiting when he came to a stop. She tapped on the window, and he rolled it down. She plunged her hands into her jacket pockets and looked up sheepishly.

"I feel like a real dope, but I haven't got enough money with me after all, so would you settle for an omelette at my place?"

"Sounds good."

"It's not far. I live on Lake of the Isles."

"I'll follow you."

She shivered, ran back to her van, and twenty minutes later the headlights of his car followed hers into the driveway between the high snowbanks.

When she emerged from the depths of the dark garage, he was waiting to lower the door for her, and once again Allison was struck by his unfailing good manners. He performed each courtesy with a naturalness that most men seemed to have long forgotten in this day of women's independence. Allison felt special when he treated her in this gentlemanly way. Inwardly she chuckled as she led the way up the stairway to her apartment, realizing she was dressed more like a combat soldier than a lady. Yet he still afforded her chivalry at every opportunity. And he did it in so offhand a manner as to make her feel foolish for giving it a second thought.

They stamped the snow off their boots and walked into her gaily decorated apartment. He was already pulling off his boots before she could turn around to protest, "Oh, you don't have to."

But he tugged them off anyway, then stood looking around the room while she removed her jacket and waited for his.

"Hey, this is like a touch of summer. You do all this yourself?" he asked.

"Yes. I like green, as you can see."

"Me too." His eyes scanned the room, moving from

item to item while he shrugged from his jacket and absently handed it to her. "You have a nice touch. Looks to me like if you ever wanted to give up photography, you could take up interior decorating."

"Thank you, but you're making me blush. Please, just . . . just sit down and make yourself at home."

One brow raised, he glanced back over his shoulder with a grin to see if she was really blushing, but she was busy hanging up their jackets in a small closet behind the door.

She turned, caught him grinning at her, and gave him a little shove toward the living room. "Go . . . sit down or something. I'll be right back."

While she was gone, he walked around the room, noticing the tape player, the healthy plants, the daybed out on the closed-off sun porch. The main room was marvelous, full of light and color, its rich wood floor gleaming, tasteful art prints in chrome frames hanging on the walls. A decorator easel stood in one corner, and he wondered why it was empty. Hands in pockets, he ambled over to the opposite corner and was gazing at the ceiling hook that held up the suspended chair when she returned to the room.

"Doubting Thomas?" she inquired archly.

He glanced over his shoulder. She had put on some lip gloss and combed her hair. On her feet were huge, blue fuzzy slippers. "You read my mind so easily, do you?"

"Everybody who comes in here goes over to that chair, looks up, and asks 'Will this thing really hold me?' "

"Not me. I didn't ask."

"No, but you were about to."

"No, I wasn't."

She went to the kitchen end of the room and opened the refrigerator, in search of eggs. Funny, she had an inkling he'd ask it, even before he asked it.

"Hey, will this thing hold me?"

But he was already inserting himself into the almost circular basket, but very, very gingerly, as if it were going to drop him the moment he settled his full weight in it.

"Nope!" she answered.

He laughed, crossed his hands over his belly, pushed gently with his heel, and called across the room, "Hey, I want an under-duck."

"A what?" she asked, popping her head up from the depths of the cabinet where she was searching for a bowl.

"An under-duck. You know . . . when you were a little kid and you got pushed on a swing, didn't you call it an under-duck when they'd go running right under you?"

"Oh, *that!*" She laughed, cracked the eggs into the bowl, and remembered back. "No, I think we used to call it . . ." She screwed up her face, trying to remember.

"Would you believe I can't think of what we used to call it."

"Shame on you. How will you teach your kids those all-important things if you forget them yourself?"

"Haven't got any kids."

From the depths of the basket chair Rick studied her while she beat the eggs with a wire whisk. The movement made her shining hair bounce at the ends, and inside her baggy sweatshirt he could make out the outline of her breasts bouncing, too. He let his glance rove down to her derrière—tiny, shapely buns . . . trim hips . . . long, supple legs.

You will have kids, he decided, admiring what he saw. "Do you plan to have kids?" he asked.

"Not for a while. I've got a career to establish first. I'm just getting up a good head of steam."

He liked the way she moved, brisk and sure, taking a moment to wipe her palms on her thighs before reaching into the cabinet for a salt shaker.

Allison was conscious of his eyes following her, though she wasn't even facing him. It was disconcerting, yet welcome in a way, too. She was standing uncertainly, gazing into an open cabinet as she admitted, "This is awful, but all I have to put in an omelette is tuna fish."

She turned apologetically to find him six inches behind her. Startled, she drew back a step.

"Tuna-fish omelette?" he repeated, grimacing. "You lured me up here for a tuna-fish omelette?"

"I didn't lure you up here, and besides, experimentation is the mother of invention."

"I thought that was necessity."

"Well . . . whatever." She gestured haplessly. "Right now it's necessary for me to experiment, all right?"

"Okay, tuna-fish omelette. I'll grin and bear it, but we could have had a perfectly good hamburger and french fries if you hadn't been so stubborn."

"I get that way sometimes . . . female pride or something like that." She turned her back on him and rummaged for a can opener, her heart fluttering giddily at his nearness. When the tuna can was open, he reached around her, took a pinch, and popped it into his mouth. "Sorry," he offered, without the least note of contrition in his voice, "but I'm starving, and I thought I'd get at least one good taste before you ruin it."

"Would you rather have a tuna sandwich?" But immediately she waggled her palms. "No, forget I asked that. I just remembered I'm out of bread."

"There's one thing a person can't accuse you of, and that's trying to finagle your way to a man's heart through his stomach." He turned away and wandered to the tape deck, squatting down on his haunches to scan the titles on the shelf below. "You like The Five Senses, huh?" he noted.

At his question something tight and constricting

seemed to settle across Allison's chest. A lump formed in her throat as she stared, unseeing, at Rick's back.

He swung around on the balls of his feet to look at her, and immediately she whirled to face the cabinet. "Yeah," she said, so crisply the word held an edge of ice.

Immediately he sensed he'd touched a nerve. She exuded defensiveness that chilled him clear across the room. "Do you mind if I put something on?"

She stared at the frying pan, seeing Jason Ederlie instead, wondering how she'd react if Rick happened by accident to put on the wrong song. Yet she'd just said she liked The Five Senses, so how could she possibly say what she was thinking: *anything* but The Five Senses.

"Go ahead," she answered lifelessly, leaving him to wonder what motivated her quicksilver change of mood.

She busied herself with the omelette, and a few minutes later the music of Melissa Manchester drifted through the apartment. Relieved, she cast him a quick glance to find he was standing by the stereo, studying her across the room.

Don't ask, she begged silently. *Don't ask, please.* Thankfully, he didn't, but went to sit on the davenport and wait to be called to the table. He stretched out, crossed his feet at the ankles, threaded his fingers together, and hung them over his belly, watching her covertly as she put the food on the table and wondering what had caused her sudden defensiveness.

A guy, he supposed. When it involved music it was usually a guy and some song the two of them had considered special. He made a mental note never to play any of The Five Senses tapes if he ever got up here again.

"It's ready," she announced soberly, standing beside the table with a long face.

He eased slowly to his feet, walked across the room, and stood by a chair next to hers. "Listen, I'm sorry for whatever I said that upset you. Whatever it was, I'm sorry."

Her lips parted slightly, and for a moment she looked as if she might cry. Then she slipped her hands into her jeans pockets, her throat working convulsively. "It's not your fault, okay?" she offered softly. "It's just something I have to get over, that's all."

His sober eyes rested on her questioningly, but he asked nothing further. Wordlessly he leaned across the corner of the table to pull out her chair. "Agreed. Now sit down so I can, too."

She gave him a shaky smile and sat, but the gaiety had evaporated from the evening. They shared their meal in strained silence, as if another presence were in the room separating them.

Allison avoided Rick's eyes as he intermittently

studied her, the downcast mouth, the forlorn droop of shoulder. His eyes moved to her left hand—no ring. Covertly they moved around the room in search of evidence of a man sharing the place or having shared it. There were no pictures, magazines, articles of any kind intimating a male presence in her life. His gaze moved to her again, to her shapely mouth, breasts, fine-boned jaw, shell-like ears, downcast eyes, and slender hand picking disinterestedly at the omelette. He leaned toward her slightly, resting his forearms on the edge of the table.

"Stop me if I'm stepping on hallowed ground," he began, "but are you committed to someone?"

Her head snapped up, and a shield seemed to drop over her eyes.

"Yes." She dropped her fork, giving up all pretense of eating. "To myself."

A brief flare of anger shone in his eyes. "That's not what I meant, and you know it. Is there some man in your life right now?"

Her heart began to beat furiously, but immediately memories of Jason came to quell it. "No," she answered truthfully, "and I don't want one."

He scrutinized her silently for a moment, his lips compressed. "Fair enough, but I had to ask. I enjoyed myself tremendously the last two evenings." He watched her carefully while relaxing back in his chair, leaning his elbows on the chrome armrests.

She propped her elbows beside her plate, entwined her fingers, and rested her forehead against white thumb knuckles. A shaky sigh escaped her lips. "I did too, but that's as far as it goes."

"Is it?"

"Yes!" she snapped, but her eyes remained hidden while her lips trembled.

"Somebody hurt you, and you're going to make damn sure nobody does again."

"It's none of your business!" Her shoulders stiffened, and her head came up.

"We'll see," he said with disarming certainty, not a flicker of doubt in his unsmiling countenance.

"I make it a practice never to get personally involved with my models. I'm sorry if you thought . . ." Her eyelids fluttered self-consciously before her gaze fell to her plate. "I mean, I never meant to lead you on."

"You didn't. You've been a lady every inch of the way, all right?"

Her eyes met his again—unsteady brown to steady blue. Against her will Allison was struck again by his flawless handsomeness, even as it filled her with mistrust. She wanted to believe he was sincere, perhaps for a moment. His face wore a look of quiet determination, warning her that he wouldn't back off without a fight.

She swallowed. "It's been a long day—"

"Say no more, I'm gone." Immediately he was on his feet, plate in hand, heading for the sink.

She felt small and guilty for giving him such an obvious brush-off when he'd been a perfect gentleman. But since Jason her instinct for self-preservation was finely honed. The faster she got Rick Lang out of here, the better.

He padded over to the entry, picked up a boot, and leaned his backside against the door while pulling it on. From the closet she retrieved his coat, and before she realized what she was doing, held it out as she'd often done for Jason. A surprised expression flitted across Rick's face before he turned, slipped his arms in, and faced her once more, slowly closing the snaps while she waited uncomfortably for him to finish and leave.

She trained her eyes on the frayed collar, afraid to raise them further, for she knew he was studying her while the sound of the snaps seemed to tick away the strained seconds.

His hands reached the last one, and he leisurely tugged his gloves from the jacket pocket, slowly pulled them on while she stared at them, knowing no other place to safely rest her eyes. He jammed his spread fingers into the gloves, all the while studying her averted face.

He was dressed for outside, ready to go, yet he stood there without making a motion toward the door.

"I heard what you said before. I know what you were telling me," he said in a low voice. "But I just have to do this . . ."

She had a vague impression of the scent of leather while his glove tipped her chin up. Soft, warm, slightly opened lips touched hers. A tongue tip briefly flicked. Two strong gloved hands squeezed her upper arms, pulling her upward, forcing her to her toes momentarily, catching her totally off guard. Almost as if it were a harbinger of things to come, the kiss ended with a slow separation of their mouths. He lifted his head, studying her eyes for a brief moment, then dropped his gaze to her surprised, open lips.

"Nice," he said softly. Then he was gone, leaving behind only a rush of cold air and a trembling in her stomach.

Chapter
FIVE

ALLISON half expected Rick to call the following
day, Wednesday, but he didn't. She wondered
what he'd say when he walked into the studio
Thursday night. She wondered how to act, then decided
she would act no differently than she had all along.
Maintaining the same light, teasing banter would be the
best way to remain at ease and keep their relationship on
a nonpersonal level.

One of Allison's Wednesday chores was to talk her
landlord out of a garden hose and lug it up to the studio
in preparation for filling the "lake." Then she made a
trip to get firewood and a piece of asbestos for under it,
so the heat wouldn't raise the linoleum off the studio
floor. If that night watchman found out she was going to

start a fire in the middle of the building, she'd be out on her ear. Thankfully the building was such a relic it had no smoke alarm or sprinkler system.

Thursday she filled the pool, checking to make sure there were no leaks, then set up her lights, deciding how many she'd need, the general positioning of both key light and fill lights, and what color filters to use on each. She cut out a circle in the backdrop paper, inserted an orange filter on one of the strobes, and positioned it to simulate the moon, which would appear only as a hazy, out-of-focus orb in the finished photograph, its reflection on the water being the chief reason she needed it at all.

By five o'clock she was loading her camera with nervous fingers, telling herself this was stupid, this was business, and Rick Lang was only a model.

Then why was she shaking?

She secured the camera on its tripod, coiled up the hose, disconnected it from the bathroom faucet, then cursed softly to find it had left a trail of water across the floor. Mopping up the spill, she suddenly remembered she hadn't asked the janitor for a wet vac to have on hand in case of an emergency, and ran to do so.

Returning to the studio, pushing the clumsy machine, Allison found Rick standing in front of the set, studying it.

He looked up as she entered and smiled.

"Hi," he said simply.

Something joyfully warm and appreciative crept along her veins at the sight of him. It was impossible to forget his brief parting kiss.

"Hi."

"You did it." He grinned, glancing at the lake, the sand, the bonfire ready for lighting.

"I told you I would." She sauntered over to the edge of the set.

"Clever lighting, with the moon—I presume—reflecting across the water." He turned to indicate the strobe showing through the backdrop, the low positioning of the camera on the tripod.

"Let's hope so. We haven't taken the shots or seen the results yet."

"How did you get that lake filled up?"

"With a garden hose."

"And you're going to suck it up with that when you're done?" He indicated the wet vac.

"Yup." She flipped her palms up and gave him a plucky smile. "Simple."

"Don't underrate yourself. It's more than simple, it's ingenious." Glancing at the set again he commented, "I see you made another trip for firewood."

"Yup."

"Who carried you out this time?" he teased.

"I wore my boots like a good girl. How 'bout you? Did you bring your bathing trunks?"

"Yup!" He pulled them out of a pocket, rolled up

tight. "Got 'em right here, but I'm not anxious to put 'em on. It's like a meat locker in here, as usual."

"Don't worry, the fire will warm you up."

"Oh, I thought Vivien Zucchini was supposed to do that." He grinned down at Allison, hooked his thumbs in the pockets of his letter jacket, and watched her swing away.

"Zuchinski," she corrected without turning around.

Rick grinned in amusement, watching her trim hips and thighs take no-nonsense steps. Her hair swayed. Her backside was firm and athletic as she strode toward the dressing-room doorway, reached inside, and flipped the lights on. Slipping her hands into the pockets of her slacks, she turned and leaned one shoulder against the dressing-room doorway like a model in a chic shampoo ad. He scanned her long-sleeved khaki safari jacket, which was belted and had epaulets at the shoulders, his eyes lingering only a fraction of a second on the breast pockets with their button-down flaps. Matching trousers were tucked into thigh-high boots. Her hair was again held behind her ears by the upraised sunglasses, though night had fallen outside and inside the lights were dim.

"I've had the door to the dressing room closed so it would warm up in there," she said. "I don't want you to freeze and break in half before we get you posed and the fire started."

"Where's Miss Zucchini?"

She laughed, hands still in pockets, bending forward

at the waist, then peering at him with mock admonishment. "If you say that one more time, she's going to walk in here and I'm going to pour tomato sauce over her instead of oil!"

Rick leaned back and laughed appreciatively while Allison checked her wristwatch. "She's due any minute. If you want to use the dressing room first, we can get started oiling you."

The oiling was news to him, though it was common practice to oil skin to simulate wetness and bring out highlights on the skin.

But at that moment the door opened and in came a stunning blue-eyed brunette bundled up to her ears in fake fur. In an affronted tone she said, "I hope it's warmer in here than it was the other day, or my unmentionables will shrivel up like raisins."

Both Rick and Allison burst out laughing. The woman gazed at them with wide, innocent eyes, as if she had no idea she'd made a graceless, tasteless opening remark.

"Rick Lang, I'd like you to meet Vivien Zuchinski." It was all Allison could do to hold a straight face and get the name right. "Vivien, this is Rick Lang, the man you'll be posing with."

Rick extended his hand.

In slow, sultry motion, Vivien's came out to meet it. She wrapped it tightly in long, shapely fingers with long, shapely nails of a ghastly vermilion that looked surprisingly right on her. Sweeping her spaghetti-length lashes up and down Rick's body, Vivien cooed, "Ooooo, *nice*."

Rick laughed good-naturedly, playing along when Vivien refused to relinquish his hand. "Likewise, I'm sure, Vivien," he said congenially. "I'm happy to share a book cover with a pretty face like yours."

She teased the hairs on the back of his hand with a tapered nail and widened her devastating eyes on him. "Heyyyy, no . . . lisssen, I'm the one that's really knocked out. I mean, you're really somethin', Rick. I'm already forgetting how cold it is in here."

Allison cleared her throat, and Vivien turned to find her leaning against the doorway to the dressing room, one foot crossed in front of the other, with a toe to the floor.

"Mr. Lang has been complaining about how cold it is in here, too, so maybe the two of you can warm each other up, huh?" Bringing her shoulder away from the door frame, Allison gestured Vivien into the brightly lit dressing room. "Would you like to be first, Miss Zook—" She caught herself just in time and finished, "Miss Zuchinski?"

Vivien swooped into the dressing room, shedding her coat and looking around. "Heyyyy, *nice*. Lots of good light for putting on makeup."

"Yours looks great already, so don't change a thing. Just put on your suit, and I'll give you a bottle of baby oil. Is your hair naturally curly?"

"What?" Vivien momentarily gave up studying her pouting lips in the mirror.

"Your hair—is it naturally curly? I'd like to put baby oil on it, too, to create the illusion of wetness."

Vivien patted her tresses with deep concern. "Oil! On my hair? I'd rather not."

"How about just on the ends then, to make it look like you've been in the water?"

"Well, you're the boss . . . but, gee!" She looked crestfallen, her face much more expressive than her vocabulary.

"Why don't you change first, then we'll experiment a little," Allison advised.

Vivien closed the door all but a crack, through which she waggled two fingers at Rick before closing it the rest of the way. Allison bit her lip to keep from laughing, but she couldn't resist glancing Rick's way to check his reaction. When their eyes met, he feigned a wolfish grin and rubbed his palms together in anticipation. "Hey, I can't wait," he teased in a whisper.

"I'll just bet you can't."

The door opened a short time later, and Vivien appeared, clad in a minuscule two-piece bathing suit that showed off every voluptuous hill and valley to great advantage. Out she came, hands thrown wide. "How's this?"

"Wow!" Rick exclaimed exuberantly.

"Nice," Allison commented dryly.

"I'm ready for oiling," Vivien declared.

"Let me get the tomato sauce, and I'll get you started," Allison quipped.

"The wha-a-a-t?" Vivien questioned, a puzzled frown on her face, dropping her hands to her hips.

"Rick, go ahead and change," Allison suggested. "It's just an old inside term, Vivien. Come on."

Allison felt rather small, having resorted to such catty tactics with Vivien. It wasn't like her at all. What in the world had she been thinking to say such a thing? Vivien was here as a professional, and if anyone was acting unprofessional, it was Allison herself. The truth was, Vivien Zuchinski was a beautiful woman with impressive proportions. Allison was abashed to find herself slightly jealous.

In two minutes the changing-room door opened again. "Hey, come on in, ladies, it's warmer in here."

Standing behind her desk, Allison lifted her eyes, and her mouth went dry. Rick stood in the doorway, barefooted, bare chested, bare legged, only that tight white suit striping his midsection, dividing his dark skin. Unlike Vivien, he didn't flaunt his assets, but just appeared at the door, invited them in, then stepped inside himself.

"Heyyyy, sugar, I'm comin'!" Vivien giggled.

There was an awkward moment when Allison stepped to the door and handed Rick a full bottle of baby oil. Her eyes had lost all hint of teasing. He was magnificent! Sparkling golden hair covered not only his chest, but also dove in a thin line down his belly, covering his legs and arms lightly. He turned to face the mirror and poured a modicum of oil into his palm, then began applying it to his shoulders while Allison saw his back for the first time. Her eyes drifted from wide shoulders to narrow hips, taking in firm skin and fine-toned muscle. His derrière was flat, his legs well shaped without the bulging muscles that ruined the male form when it came to photographing it. Truly, his body was an artist's concept of beauty.

In the mirror Allison caught his eye and knew he'd been watching her assess him, but he only looked away and continued applying oil briskly. Unlike Jason, who used every such opportunity to smirk and flaunt and tease with his eyes, Rick accepted his physical assets with dignity, but not ego. He radiated no sexy innuendo, but merely turned to the mirror and vigorously continued what he was doing.

Vivien sat on a chair and hooked her shapely toes— vermilion, too, Allison noted—on the edge of the vanity, squirting a line of oil up a perfect leg. Spreading it, she kept her eyes on Rick.

"I'll put some on your back," Allison offered, moving behind Vivien, who swiveled sideways a little on the chair.

It seemed Vivien had dreams of becoming a Playboy

bunny, and she prattled on about a trip she had taken to the Playboy Club in Chicago, all the while scouring Rick with admiring gazes.

"I think we'll need some oil on the ends of your hair anyway, Vivien. Do you want me to put it on?" Allison asked.

"Do we have to?" Again Vivien appeared devastated.

"Unless you have some other suggestion as to how we can make it appear wet."

Vivien stood before the giant mirror beside Rick, leaning forward while she concentrated on the monumental decision, then began applying carefully controlled amounts of oil to selected strands of hair.

"Will you help me with my back?" Rick asked Allison, offhandedly passing the bottle of oil over his shoulder and catching her eyes in the mirror.

She was suddenly reluctant to lay a hand on him. She had little choice, however, and accepted the bottle from his slippery fingers. Thank God he didn't grin or tease, just handed the bottle over and waited. Allison poured oil into her palm, thinking: This is how it all started with Jason.

She went at it energetically to hide the fact that her hand shook when she touched Rick's bare skin for the first time. She was unaware of how she glowered or that behind closed lips she held the tip of her tongue tightly between her teeth. Sensations of touch came flooding back to her, filling her memory and her body at this first touch of a man's flesh since Jason's. How many times had she done this for him? How many times had he done this to her? How many times had their oiled skins delighted each other?

Don't think about Jason. Don't think about the fragrance of the oil. Don't think about all the times he was sleek and slippery and seductive.

But Rick's flesh beneath Allison's hand was warm and firm, and her palm slipped over it, conforming to its strong, sleek lines. The shoulder was tough, the shoulder blade hard, the neck unyielding with a tensile strength. Her fingertips inadvertently touched Rick's hair and learned its fine softness, so different from the hardness of his muscles. The contrast jolted her, and she raised her eyes to the mirror to find Rick studying her solemnly.

She was suddenly swept with the awkward feeling that he'd read her mind. Immediately she dropped her eyes to his back again. Taking more oil, she worked it down the warm center of his back to the waistband of his trunks. The memory of his light, undemanding kiss came back to her, and his words, "I just have to do this." With her hands on his skin he somehow became all mixed up in her mind with Jason. Love, hurt, sensuality, and bitterness welled up within Allison, leaving her confused. Then her fingertips slipped over Rick's ribs, and he flinched and tipped guardedly sideways.

Allison came back to the present, realizing it was Rick, not Jason. Their eyes met in the mirror.

"I'm ticklish," he informed her, and the spell was—thankfully—broken.

"I'll remember next time." She handed him the bottle, said, "Excuse me," and reached around him for a roll of paper towels on the vanity.

"Your hair, too," she instructed, brushing alarmingly close to his chest as she reached.

"What?"

Wiping her hands gave her an excuse not to look up at his reflection in the mirror. "Oil your hair, too. How're you doing, Vivien?"

"Can't say I like getting all greasy like this, but I hear oil makes the hair healthy, huh?"

"As soon as you two are done, come on out to the set. I'll get the lighting started."

Outside the wide wall of windows it was totally black. Inside, the only light came from the dressing room. Allison shook off thoughts of Rick Lang and set to work, adjusting the direction of the strobes, firing them time after time to see the effect they created on log, water, sand. Working with a light meter, she took readings from various points, adjusting the rheostats on individual strobes, which were all connected to a single triggering device that would fire them simultaneously with the shutter release when connected to the camera.

Rick and Vivien padded out, barefoot and shivering,

to find Allison's shadowy form darting back and forth amid the equipment.

"Oh, good, you're ready. Listen, this sounds like a joke, but I have to crack a window a little bit to let the smoke out once I start the fire. But the room should warm up as soon as the fire gets going. I'm really sorry about the chill in here, but bear with me, okay? I didn't want to strike the match until you two were out here, because I don't want that fire going any longer than necessary.

"Okay, Rick, I want you on the log, Vivien laying on the sand below him, facing him and rather leaning up onto his outstretched leg, gazing up into his face. For now, take the general positions, but don't strain yourselves to hold them. Just relax and I'll light the fire and do a final metering on all the strobes once the flame is going."

A shivering Vivien moved toward the set, rubbing her goose-pimpled arms.

"Step lightly on that sand," Allison warned, "and move slowly across it so it doesn't get spread out any more than necessary." Vivien's teeth were chattering. "Rick, why don't you sit down on the log first?" Allison continued. "Maybe Vivien can lean against your legs for a minute and keep warm." There was no joking now in Allison's voice. As Vivien picked her way gingerly across the sand, Allison touched a match to the hidden chunk of Dura-Flame log that gave a clean, smokeless *pouff* before the small twigs caught. Immediately Allison was moving about, taking readings, firing the strobes time and time again, resetting the angle of the camera now that she had bodies to compose in the viewfinder. Crouching, she peered into the camera to assess the angle of the moon's reflection on the water, firing the strobes repeatedly, making minute adjustments.

The oil caught the gleam of the strobes and sent it shimmering to the eye of the camera, creating precisely the illusion of wetness Allison was aiming for. She decided it would not be necessary to further discomfort Rick and Vivien by sprinkling water on their already shivering skin. In the night light the oil was all that was necessary.

The key light had a blue filter to simulate moonlight. When Allison fired it, Rick's hair took on a life of its own, haloed to perfection in all its glorious disarray. Vivien's, too, became a moonlit nimbus about her head, the oiled ends perfect.

By using fill lights with orange filters, Allison had eliminated shadows that were too stark, tempering them with simulated firelight at each flash.

"Okay, all set," she declared, moving toward the set now, standing just beyond the sand, leaning over with hands on thighs, giving orders. She positioned Rick with his far knee raised slightly, the near leg stretched out with only its heel resting on the sand. Touching his shoulders, she ordered, "Turn . . . no, not so much . . . good. Now tip that head down, and Vivien, I want you to look like you want to crawl right up his body. Roll onto your far hip just a little . . . a little more, let me see just a hint of tummy. Good, now brace on your left hand any way you can to keep from falling over, and put your right hand on his chest." There followed a single reflex drawing them apart as Vivien's biceps inadvertently came up against Rick's vitals, for she lay in the vee of his legs now. But the two of them reverted to faultless professionalism in an instant, settling into the pose again.

Allison produced a small jar of petroleum jelly, touched a spot of it to the corner of Vivien's mouth, produced a comb from her pocket, and tugged free a strand of Vivien's beautiful hair to fasten to the corner of her lips. Perfect!

"There . . . don't move," Allison breathed, backing away. Immediately she returned, touched the comb to a few wayward strands of hair at the back of Rick's neck, flicked it through a lock above his ear to partially cover the top of it, then stepped to the camera to evaluate the composition in the viewfinder. Immediately she saw sand where it wasn't supposed to be, produced a small, soft barber's brush and whisked it off the top of Vivien's leg. Another check in the viewfinder, a flash of strobes, and she found the stunning fire glow had created exactly the skin effect she wanted. But the sand that she'd found distracting on Vivien seemed lacking on Rick. Quickly she stepped around the tripod, picked up a handful and threw it at his near shoulder.

This time the scene in the viewfinder was flawless. Another quick check of all the strobes, firing them six times in quick succession before connecting them to synchronize with the camera.

Allison's voice became silk as she stepped behind the camera, crouching low, ready to shoot.

"All right, I want you to think about that skin you're touching . . . sleek, desirable . . . wet those lips, come on." Their tongues came out, leaving lips glossy in the firelight. The strobes flashed as the shutter opened for the first time, capturing the image on film. Allison's heart hammered with excitement. They were perfect together!

"Ease up a little higher, Vivien, and droop those eyelids just a li-i-i-i-tle more . . . more . . . no, too far, lift your chin now, think of how much you love him."

Flash!

"Great!" Exhilaration filled Allison as she moved deftly around the camera, giving sharp orders at times, soft compelling orders at others.

"Rick, I want a long, caressing thumb touching the hair that's caught in her mouth, but don't cover those beautiful lips of hers . . . let my camera see them . . .

good with the thumb, now closer with your lips . . . think about tongues . . ."

Flash!

"Let's see the tip of your tongue, Vivien, and ease up with that hand on his chest. You're caressing it, not hanging suspended from it."

The perfection broke and both Rick and Vivien laughed, falling out of their poses momentarily.

Allison waited only briefly before saying, "Okay, back at it, lovers. Let's get messages going between those eyes, and Vivien, I want that tongue peeking out . . . open the teeth only slightly . . . good, good."

Flash!

"All right, Rick, spread those fingers and bury them in her hair . . . you love that magnificent hair, you're lost in it . . . not so deep, we're losing those beautiful fingers of yours, gently . . . gently."

Flash!

"You have wonderful hands, Rick. Let's use them some more, give me sensuality with your hands . . . wing it, fly with it, Vivien, respond to his every touch . . ."

Rick relaxed, curled his fingers, and lay the knuckles gently against the crest of Vivien's cheek. At his touch she turned her head slightly as if to take more, lips falling open, eyelids drooping with sensuality.

Flash!

"Now you, Vivien, what can you do with those delicate fingers . . . touch him where he wants to be

touched, turn him on, tell him with your fingertips
what's on your mind. . . ."

Vivien's hands slid down to Rick's bare thigh, and
immediately his face reacted. His shoulders and arms
spoke to the camera of wanting to express more than the
photograph would allow.

They continued for a series of twenty-four shots, and
during that time Allison all but forgot who Vivien
Zuchinski and Rick Lang were. She moved with an unconscious purity of purpose and saw her subjects with
uncanny acuity, missing not one hair that needed
straightening or messing. Halfway through the first roll
of film she repositioned Vivien, raising her farther up
until her head rested against Rick's chest. Ordering Rick
to place his hand almost on the side of Vivien's breast,
hers on his hip, she received an immediate, professional
response, then hustled back to the camera.

Rick and Vivien were subjects, integral parts of the
art she created, nothing less. Allison's vitality and enthusiasm brought out the best in them, and her businesslike attitude put both Rick and Vivien at ease in a
situation that otherwise might have been embarrassing.

When it was time to change film, Allison straightened. "Okay, stretch for a minute, but watch that sand—
don't get it anyplace I don't want it."

She fetched fresh film from the old refrigerator and
in a matter of minutes had reloaded. A quick check of
the fire, another stick on it, and it was back to work.

They resumed shooting, with Allison issuing rapid-fire orders that immediately brought changes of pose, expression, and body language. With the next change of film came a change of camera angle. This time Allison posed Rick and Vivien hip to hip, facing each other, creating sensuality not only with near kisses, but with hands on each other's ankles and calves. Another pose had Rick leaning across Vivien's lap, his lips just above the fullest part of her breast while her head hung back in abandon.

As the session moved on, the models' muscles grew stiff, and, quite naturally, their facial expression and body language did, too. Allison worked quickly, efficiently, noting the first times Rick and Vivien sighed wearily, understanding that cramps and outright pain were very real afflictions for models.

But when Vivien suddenly jumped and raised her backside sharply off the sand, ruining a shot, Allison's head popped out from behind the camera.

"Tired, Vivien?"

"No, something bit me." She scratched the underside of a thigh, then settled back into the pose again.

But just as Allison pushed the shutter release again, Rick twitched, ruining a second shot.

"You two need a break?"

"No," they answered in unison.

"Let's keep going and get finished," Rick advised. "All right, Vivien?" He gave her a considerate glance.

"Sure, this sand is . . . ouch!" This time Vivien leapt to her feet.

Now Allison became concerned. What was troubling Vivien?

"You too?" Rick questioned, suddenly getting to his feet and straining around, twisting at the waist in an attempt to see the backs of his thighs. "I could swear something's been having me for dinner, but I didn't want to say anything."

"Honey, you and me both!" Vivien seconded, scratching her legs now, lifting one foot to rake her nails on the back of an ankle.

Allison stepped to the light switch. A moment later the room was flooded with light while she knelt at the edge of the fake beach, studying the sand. She could see nothing. She fetched a large white sheet of paper and laid it on the sand, stooping again to watch carefully. A moment later she saw a tiny black dot hit the paper and disappear so fast her eyes couldn't follow.

Horrified, she stood up, biting her lip. "I hope you two have a good sense of humor, because it looks like sand fleas."

"Sand fleas!" Vivien yelped. "Eating *me?*"

"I'm afraid so. They must have come to life when the heat from the fire thawed them out." Immediately Vivien began scratching harder. "I'm . . . I'm really sorry about this," Allison apologized, more than a little embarrassed. Lord, what next! she thought. How was she going to control the insects and finish the rest of the shots? There was no bug spray in the studio. Crestfallen, Allison added, "I don't have anything to get rid of the pesky things. I guess we'll have to stop shooting and go with what we have. Hey, I'm really sorry."

"How many shots do you have left on that roll?" Rick inquired.

Allison checked. "Thirteen."

Rick turned to Vivien. "Well, I can stand it for thirteen more if you can. What do you say, Vivien?"

Suddenly Vivien grinned, and with a rueful gesture said, "Ah, what the heck. Fleas have to eat, too."

To Allison's surprise, they resumed their places and suffered through the rest of the shots with the best of humor.

"Ah, that one likes his steak rare," Rick joked.

"I would too if I could take a bite out of the back of your leg," Vivien countered.

"Do you suppose we should demand to see a certificate from the local exterminator before setting foot in this place again?"

"To say nothing of the fire marshal."

"I think maybe an extra life-insurance policy is in order before taking a job at Photo Images. How about you, Vivien?"

"Why, whatever makes you ask? I have a bad case of

pneumonia, slivers in my back from this log, flea bites, and my feet are scorching!"

"All right, you two . . . that's it!" Allison announced, ending the session.

By this time it was almost ten o'clock, and they were all grateful to stretch and bend. As the overhead fluorescent lights came on, Allison rejoiced, "A hundred and fifty-four shots, and you two were fabulous!"

"I think she's soothing our egos in hopes we won't sue for damages," Rick kidded as he and Vivien hurried off the sand.

"Damn pesky things!" Vivien exclaimed, dancing, scratching again.

"I really am sorry, and I mean that. You were both . . ." Allison searched for the proper word. "Intrepid!"

Vivien, looking puzzled, turned to Rick and asked, "Is she sayin' I didn't do so hot?"

They all laughed. "You were great, and I mean that sincerely," Allison clarified. She had gained a new, healthy respect for the girl who—true—might not be exceptionally bright. But she had a glow that looked wonderful through the viewfinder and, more important, a willingness and tenacity, even under less than ideal conditions. Allison had worked with lots of models who grew increasingly irritable as their muscles tightened and the hours passed. Who knew what would happen if they were asked to pose in a nest of sand fleas! But throughout it all Vivien had remained adamantly good humored and uncomplaining. "I know a lot of models who *would* sue!" Allison commented.

"Only thing that'll make me sue is if you don't let me get this oil off. I feel like a regular grease ball!" Vivien complained volubly, now that the session was over.

"Go ahead, you deserve it," Allison said. "Straight through the dressing room to the shower. There are clean washcloths and towels back there and plenty of soap."

Vivien disappeared through the dressing room, and Rick watched Allison remove the camera from the tripod, rewind the final roll of film, then begin disconnecting cables, pushing lights aside, seeing to the equipment.

"Can I help?"

"Absolutely not. You've done enough already." She placed a lens cap on the camera. Looking up, she found him carefully scrutinizing her. Immediately she dropped her eyes to her work. Now that the camera was no longer before her eye, it was too easy to view Rick Lang as a man instead of a model.

Just as Allison had gained a healthy respect for Vivien, Rick had gained the same for Allison. She was a true professional, with an attitude and ability that made working with her a rewarding experience.

"Hey, you're shivering," she said, and Rick snapped out of his reverie. She was wrapping an electrical cord around her arm with brisk, efficient movements.

"Am I?"

"Yeah. Why don't you see if you can find a robe in the dressing room until the shower's free?"

Instead he moved across the space between them, taking the cord from her arm while she protested, "Hey, I can—"

"So can I. Don't be so bullheaded and independent."

"But you must be tired." Somehow she acquiesced without realizing it.

"Yup, I am tired. How about you?"

"In a way, but whenever I finish a session that's gone particularly well, like this one has, I'm so high I can't come down for hours. I'll go home and feel like I'm falling off my feet, but when my head hits the pillow it'll take forever to fall asleep."

"You do love it, don't you?"

Suddenly their eyes met, and they forgot what they'd been doing. Allison's hands fell still.

"Yes, I do," she said, almost reverently. "There's no feeling like it in the world . . . not for me. Tonight was . . ." She glanced at the set, the shrouded equipment, the cable release in her hands. Finally her eyes came back to his. "It was unadulterated joy for me," she finished solemnly.

"You're damned good, Allison, do you know that?"

He spoke quietly, admiring the strong sense of purpose she emanated. Her love of work seemed to radiate from her glittering, eager eyes.

The softly spoken compliment went straight to her heart. She smiled, and her eyes fluttered away. He had never called her Allison before. It warmed her almost as much as his opinion and the ungushing way he'd voiced it. In all the months she'd worked with Jason, he'd never once come right out and said as much. He'd glanced at the finished products with an eyebrow cocked. But if he admired them, it was always with a hint of egoism that left Allison feeling slightly empty.

She studied Rick now, comparing him to Jason, finding him totally opposite—warm, sensitive, considerate.

"Thank you," she replied quietly, giving him the rare gift that to some comes so hard—accepting a compliment at face value, thereby lending it a value of its own. "So are you," she added softly.

Their eyes lingered on each other, and at last, unsmiling, he replied, "Thank you."

Just then Vivien came bouncing out of the dressing room, swaddled in her fake fur and looking considerably revived. "Shower's all yours, honey!" she announced, perkily strutting over to Rick. "But before I lose you, I want one real honest-to-goodness kiss out of that hundred-dollar-an-hour mouth of yours. I deserve it after all the suffering I've been through resisting it while it was half an inch away from me for four hours."

Boldly, Vivien slipped her fingers around Rick's neck and pulled his head down for an unabashedly lingering kiss.

He was taken off guard, and though Allison had a brief impression of his surprise, he acquiesced gracefully while Vivien audaciously demanded a full-fledged French kiss, holding his head until she'd received what she was after.

Looking on, Allison felt a little red around the collar, and again was bothered by a faint twinge of jealousy at the impudent woman who had no compunctions whatsoever about being so outlandishly forward.

Backing away, finally, Vivien gave Rick a sultry once over. "You are *reeeeeally* something. You ever want to get together where there's no camera lookin' on, you just give li'l Vivien a call, okay?"

Rick laughed into her upraised face, his hands resting on her waist. "Vivien, I just might take you up on that. Maybe we can compare fleabites," he managed, ending the touchy moment gracefully, with exactly the proper touch of humor.

Vivien socked him playfully on the shoulder. "Hey, I like that. I like a man with a nice bod and a good sense of humor. You're a real fox, fella." She flitted out of his arms with no more compunction than she'd flitted in. "Well . . . gotta run."

Allison, discomfited by watching Vivien's dauntless, straightforward display, turned her back on Rick as she gave the woman a one-armed hug and walked her toward the door.

"Vivien, you're marvelous to work with, and I'd like to do it again." She meant it. In spite of the past sixty seconds, which had been embarrassing, Allison meant it.

Chapter
SIX

WHEN Rick emerged from the dressing room, Vivien was gone. Allison had wet down the coals and was scooping the sodden lumps into a metal garbage can. She heard the door open and watched him cross the long, open length of the room. She attended to her chore, conscious of his eyes on her while he stood nearby with his hands in his pockets, conscious, too, of the flustering memory of Vivien's mouth demanding his to open. Throughout the shooting Allison had managed to keep her thoughts separate from her personal feelings, but with Rick standing beside her in street clothes, and after Vivien forcing that impromptu, final pose on him, Allison was suddenly at a loss, searching frantically for something to say. Her hand trembled as she dumped the last dustpan of coals and clapped the cover over the garbage can. As the tiny clang drifted away into silence, she looked up at last.

"Vivien's gone," she said inanely. Rick's hair was damp, clinging to his temples, coiling about his ears. The overhead lights reflected off his fresh-scrubbed forehead and nose, highlighting his skin.

"I know. And I'm sorry about what happened. I didn't mean to embarrass you."

Her cheeks flushed. "Oh, that's okay, it's none of my business." She frantically tried to appear busy, to disguise her discomposure. She wiped her hands on her thighs and looked around. Everything was done. "I'll clean up the rest tomorrow." She checked her watch. "Goodness, it's late! I'll get your check so you can go."

She escaped to her desk, picked up the check she'd made out while he was in the shower, and handed it to him, extending, too, her other hand in a gesture of good will.

Without taking his eyes from hers, he accepted the check with one hand, her cold palm with the other. But instead of shaking it, he held her hand firmly, refusing to relinquish it when she tugged away. She flashed him what she hoped was a dismissing smile and reiterated, "I really meant it when I said you were wonderful to work with. As soon as the transparencies come in, I'll give you a call so you can see them."

"Fine," he replied, obviously not giving a damn about transparencies as he still refused to release her hand.

His touch sent paths of fire up her arm, and she frantically raked her mind for something more to say. "M . . . maybe I'll get some extra color stats of the cover when it has the title and copy on, so you can see what the finished product looks like, too."

"Fine," he agreed disinterestedly, brushing a thumb against the back of her hand. His eyes remained fixed on hers. She knew instinctively it would not bother him in the least if he never saw the finished photos. It was becoming increasingly difficult to dream up things to say. Finally she stammered, "I . . . I'll call when the stats come in."

"And how long will that be?"

She forcibly pulled her palm from his. "Oh, maybe three months."

"Too long." He folded the check in half and creased it with his thumbnail without removing his eyes from her face.

"I'm afraid that's entirely up to New York. After the transparencies leave here, my part is done."

"That's not what I meant." With unnerving slowness he pulled a billfold from his hip pocket, inserted the payment, then tucked the billfold away again. "Thank you, though it doesn't seem right taking money for a job I've enjoyed as much as tonight's."

Common sense told her this was no time to make

jokes about Vivien or fleas or pneumonia. "You earned it, Rick," she said simply, gesturing nervously, then twisting her fingers together.

He shrugged, dropped his eyes to her desk, and still didn't move. He stood there, his weight on one foot, considering the clutter of photos, bills, lenses, filters. The old building emitted faraway nighttime sounds— the soft clang of a radiator pipe, the hum of a clock, a janitor's pail way off in the distance.

Finally Rick looked up. "I didn't have any supper, did you?" he asked.

"No." Her eyes met his, then flitted away. "But I'm all out of tuna and eggs."

A long silence followed while Allison commanded her eyes to stay off Rick, who seemed to be considering deeply as he stood before her.

"I don't want any of your damn tuna and eggs. I want to go somewhere and talk to you and get to know you."

Her startled eyes flew up. "I told you—"

"Hey, wait." He pressed open palms against the air. "A sandwich and a cup of coffee and some talk, okay? No commitments, I promise. You said yourself you're so keyed up you won't sleep if you do go home, so let me do the buying and you can bubble off your enthusiasm on me, okay?"

"Thank you, Rick, but the answer is no."

A slow grin climbed one cheek. "Would you reconsider if I threatened to sue for the fleabites?"

A quavering smile tipped her lips up, but a warning fluttered through her heart. Afraid of eventualities, afraid of letting anyone close again, afraid of being hurt as before, she drew in a sharp breath, stifling the sweet enjoyment she felt being with him.

"I think I'll have to call your bluff, and just hope you won't."

"Then just come because I ask, and because I can't sleep if I go straight home, either."

Uncertainly she stood before him, pressing her thighs hard against the edge of the desk, as if its solidity might anchor her to earth when she was so tempted to drift above it at his invitation.

His eyes fell to her tight-clenched hands, then rose to her face again. He moved around the side of the desk, captured one of her wrists, turned and towed her toward the door, affecting an injured tone. "Hey, you owe me. After I helped you lug six tons of bricks up here for that set, not to mention one illegal log, which put me in jeopardy with the law, and after almost getting pneumonia from the cold in here, as well as a bad case of fleabites. You can't put a man through all that, then refuse to have a cup of coffee with him."

"Rick, listen—"

"Listen, my ass, I'm done listening. You're coming with me." He moved decisively, retrieving her jacket from the hat tree and turning again to face her with the garment held wide, waiting.

With a sigh of resignation, she turned to slip her arms in. As she buttoned up, he hit the light switch, plunging the room into darkness, except for the vague light from the hallway, which fell through the old-fashioned glass window of the door.

He stood close behind her—too close for comfort—so, rather than turn again to face him, she reached for the doorknob. His hand moved quickly to cover hers and prevent her from turning it. Immediately she yanked free of his touch, burying her hand in a pocket. But his palms fell lightly on her shoulders, turning her to face him once more.

His fingers circled her neck, under the jacket hood, pressing on her collarbone, the thumbs pushing the wool fabric lightly against her throat. A spill of brightness from the hallway washed one side of his face, leaving the other in shadow, and Allison experienced an unruly wish to photograph him this way, for his profile was pure, sharp, perfect, the sober expression in his eyes accentuated by the fact that one eye was thrown totally into shadow.

She was conscious of the scent of soap lingering on his skin and of the warmth from his hands seeping through her coat to circle her neck.

"For some reason you don't trust me," he said softly. "I can tell it. Yet I think you enjoy being with me, and I know I enjoy being with you. I won't push—that's a promise—but neither will I give up on a relationship with definite possibilities."

"I . . . I'm not looking for a relationship. I already told you that."

"Hey." He shook her gently, cajolingly. "People don't look for relationships. They just happen, Allison, like heaven-sent gifts, don't you know that? Afterward, the two people can work on them. But meeting is the accident."

"No, I don't know any such thing." She herself had spent years, it seemed, always *looking* for a relationship, only to be wounded when she found it, and it ended just like the one before, against her wishes.

His gaze was intense as he studied her face, half-lit from the hall. She found it impossible to pull her eyes away. "What are you afraid of?" he asked, his voice gone slightly gruff.

"I'm not afraid. I just view things . . . people . . . more cynically than you do. Besides, heaven has never sent me a gift that turned out to be worth two cents, so you'll pardon me if I don't take a very optimistic view of heaven."

"Maybe I can change your mind," he ventured.

"I doubt it."

"Do you mind if I try?"

"That depends."

"On what?"

"On what you want from me."

"Why do you think I want something?"

"Everybody wants something." She swallowed. "Only they usually want it for nothing."

"Who was the last person who wanted something from you for nothing?"

"Nobody!" she retorted too sharply. Then quieter, "Nobody."

His eyes assessed her, carefully tracking the defensive expressions across her face with its downturned mouth. "You're lying," he said softly. "Somebody hurt you and left you distrusting the rest of mankind, and left me with the job of proving to you that not everyone in this world is a rat."

"You'll have a tough time doing that during the course of a quick cup of coffee."

"I believe I will," he agreed amiably, leaning around Allison to open the door. "It may take more than just tonight, but you'll find that I'm a very patient fellow." Waiting for the elevator, he asked, "Would you like to ride in my car?"

Again she watched the changing numbers above the door, knowing he was studying her. "No, I'll take the van and meet you."

"Where?"

She eyed him sideways. "Wherever we're going for coffee."

"Where would you like to go?"

She shrugged, caring only that it wasn't too dimly lit or intimate.

"Do you like big, fat, juicy hamburgers dripping with cheese and crisscrossed with bacon strips and sour pickles and fries?" He sounded like an ad for a fast-food hamburger place.

She couldn't help grinning. "I think I'm being prompted. Do *you* like big, fat, juicy hamburgers dripping with cheese and crisscrossed with bacon and dill pickles and fries?"

His eyes lit up merrily. "How'd you guess?"

"Go ahead, name it."

"The Embers—my favorite."

"And what if I said no, I don't like big, fat, juicy hamburgers, that I want a . . . a bowl of chili and a corn dog?" She pursed up her mouth in mock petulance.

"I'd say, tough! I said first, and I said hamburger. So whaddya make of it, huh, lady?" The elevator arrived and he punched her arm playfully, dancing through the open doors on the balls of his feet.

She fell back convincingly against the elevator wall. "I give!" Her hands reached for the sky. "I love hamburgers, I swear I love 'em!"

He shadowboxed his way to her, stopping close, playfully raising her chin with one gloved fist. "Yeah?" He grinned into her eyes. "Well, youse is one smart broad if youse already learned not to cross me when I want hamburgers."

By now she was laughing out loud, her shoulders shaking as she leaned against the elevator wall. He was incorrigible. If he couldn't get her one way, he got her another. It was becoming harder and harder to resist him. She found herself smiling all the way to the restaurant. Entering and scanning the booths, she found she'd arrived first.

When Rick came in minutes later, he sauntered up to her booth, leaning negligently against the backrest across from her, looked around shiftily, and asked, "Hey, ah . . . lady, ah, you're a pretty good-looker. You got anybody in particular hidin' in the men's room or somethin'?"

"That'd be tellin'," she replied in her best gun moll's accent. "With me you take your chances, bud."

Smiling, he slipped into the booth, across from her. They talked for two hours. During that time he learned she was from a small farming town in South Dakota, where her family still lived, that she'd come to Minneapolis to attend school at Communication Arts, and had stayed because the city offered opportunities for an aspiring young photographer that couldn't be found in Watertown, South Dakota. Her ambitions were to own a Hasselblad camera and to sell a fashion layout to *Gentlemen's Review* magazine.

"Why *Gentlemen's Review?*" he asked.

"Why not? It's the epitome of prestige to be published in *GR*, so why not set my goal as high as possible?"

"But why a man's magazine?"

Without thinking, she answered, "Because I'm good with men."

"Are you now?" he purred. His eyelids drooped to

half-mast, and he picked up his cup, smirking as his lips touched its rim.

She colored and stammered, "I . . . I mean with a camera, of course."

"Of course," he agreed, clearing his throat, again hiding behind his cup.

"Quit smirking and get your mind out of the gutter," she scolded, sitting up straighter. "I can see you leering behind that cup. It's the truth, I *am* good with men. I have a good eye for men's clothing and for backgrounds that flatter masculine features and for bringing out ruggedness, suaveness—whatever. I have to work much harder to achieve those things with women." She toyed with her cup. "I suppose that sounds egotistical, but it's imperative in my line of work to recognize where my strengths lie and pursue that direction."

"You're forgetting, I'm an artist, too. The same is true with my work."

She leaned forward eagerly, caught up in the subject she loved best. "It's disconcerting sometimes, isn't it, having your work so . . . so *visual!*" She gestured at the table top. "I mean, whatever we produce is right there for the world to judge us by."

They talked on about the common interest they shared. Her cheeks grew pink, her eyes excited, body language intent, and he absorbed it all with growing enjoyment.

"Do you know you become vibrant when you talk about your work?" he asked.

"I do?"

"Your cheeks get pink, and your eyes dance around, and you get all animated and turned-on looking."

She leaned back, retreating into the booth. "I guess I do. It exhilarates me."

"Like nothing else can?" The implication was clear in his voice. The memory of his kiss came back vividly, and she dropped her eyes from his carefully expressionless face. She thought it best to lighten the atmosphere. "There's one other thing that does as much for me."

"And what's that?"

"The mere thought of working with a Hasselblad." She shivered, pressing folded hands between her knees as if even the word itself were sensual.

He lifted his cup, took a sip, mentioned casually, "I own a Hasselblad."

Her eyes grew wide. Her back came away from the booth. "You do?" She gulped.

"Is that covetousness I see gleaming in your eye?"

"Is it ever!" She rolled her eyes toward the ceiling. "Oh, those enormous two-and-a-quarter-inch negatives!" she swooned. "Oh, those lenses! Oh, the dream of owning the camera the astronauts took to the moon!" She sank back as if overcome, then pressed a hand to her heart. "I'd sell my soul for one of those things."

"Sold!" he put in quickly.

"Figuratively speaking, of course. You actually own one? You're not kidding?"

"I worked one whole summer on a road-construction crew and saved every cent I possibly could, and by fall I had enough to pay for the camera."

Her face became clownishly sad. "Somehow I don't think a road-construction crew would hire me on to drive a cat."

"Don't bother applying. You can try my camera any time."

Again she sat up, surprised, a new look of fire in her eyes. "You mean that? You'd actually let me?"

He gestured nonchalantly. "I mostly use the thing when I make trips up north to Emily, where my folks live. They have a cabin on Roosevelt Lake, too, and I do most of my photography around the lake and in the woods up there. I stay in the city because the modeling pays for the wildlife art, which doesn't pay for itself yet. But, like I said, the camera's yours whenever you'd like to try it."

"You mean it, don't you?" she said, flabbergasted.

"Of course I mean it." He leaned back, crossed his arms over his chest, and hooked a boot on the seat beside her. "But I didn't offer to give it to you, just to let you try it."

She smiled, overjoyed. Her nostrils flared slightly as her eyes drifted shut for a moment. She opened them to meet his, a hint of naughtiness about her lips while she made circles around the lip of her coffee cup with an index finger.

"I might abscond with it."

They leaned back lazily, playing teasing games with half-shut eyes.

"Then I'll have to make sure I stay very close to it . . . and to you, won't I?"

Allison was suddenly very aware of his foot propped on the seat, almost touching her hip. And of how incredibly handsome he was, lazy that way, almost as if he were half asleep. And of the dancing eyes that told her he was far from asleep. And of the fact that, when the waitress asked, he had remembered she liked sugar in her coffee. And of the fact that she had laughed with him more in the last couple days than she'd laughed with Jason during all the months they'd lived together. And of the dawning realization that she and Rick Lang had an incredible lot in common.

IT was well past midnight when Rick paid their bill. Allison stood behind him, watching him shrug as he dug in his tight jeans pocket for change. His hair was flattened where he'd leaned his head against the booth. The collar of his old jacket was turned up, crinkled leather touching the back of his head. Without warning she itched to touch it, too.

Allison shook off the thought, buttoning her jacket up high and twisting her scarf twice about her neck.

"All set?" Rick asked, turning.

She nodded and moved toward the door. He reached around her, almost brushing her arm as he pushed the heavy plate glass open for her to pass through. Outside, crossing the parking lot, she was too keenly aware of the fact that he walked very near, just behind her shoulder, pulling leather gloves on while she buried her chin in her scarf, hands in pockets.

She stopped in the middle of the snow-packed parking lot and turned toward him. "Well, my car's over here."

He gestured in the opposite direction with a sideward bob of the head. "Mine's over there."

An uncertain pause followed, then, "Well, thanks for the hamburger. It was good, after all."

"Anytime."

It was quiet, late. All that could be heard were the exhaust fans on top of the restaurant humming into the neon-lit night. Allison looked up at Rick. His breath came in intermittent white clouds on the chill air. He stood before her, not a hint of smile on his face, pushing his gloves on tighter, tighter, while perusing her in the night light that turned her face pink.

"Well . . . good night," she said, hunching her shoulders against the cold.

"G'night." Still he didn't move away, but stood there studying her until she became giddily aware of how fast he was breathing. There was no hiding it, for each breath was broadcast by its spreading vapor cloud. Reactions spread through her in a warm drift of awareness.

Her heart seemed to be beating everywhere at once. Then common sense took over, and she turned quickly toward the van, only to find him still following behind her shoulder. He slipped a gloved hand on her elbow, squeezing tight as they picked their precarious way along the icy footing. Though his touch was far from intimate through layers and layers of winter clothing, it sent shivers up her spine.

At the van she reached to open the door, but he beat her to it, reaching easily around her, then standing back, waiting, with his glove on the handle.

She turned to give him a last brief glance over her shoulder.

"Well, good night and thanks again."

"Yeah," he tried, but it came out cracky, so he cleared his voice and tried again. "Yeah." Clearer this time, but low, soft, disconcerting.

Just as she was about to raise a foot and climb into the van, his hand captured her elbow once more, tugging her around.

"Allison?"

Her startled eyes met his as he circled both of her elbows with gloved hands. They stood in the narrow space between the open door and the vehicle as Rick's hands compelled her closer. The freezing night air seemed suddenly hot against her skin. He pulled her closer by degrees, his head tipping to one side, blotting out the lights behind him as his lips neared.

"Don't," she demanded at the last moment, turning aside and raising her palms to press him away, though her heartbeats were driving hard against the hollow of her throat.

The pressure on her elbows increased. "What are you afraid of?"

"You promised you wouldn't push."

"Do you call one kiss pushing?" His breath was so close it brushed her cheek, sending a cloud of warm air over her skin.

"I . . . yes," she managed, refusing to look up at him.

"Why don't you try it and see if I push any farther?" The hands commanded her again until their bodies were so close that their jackets touched. Again Allison's eyes met Rick's, which were shadows only, though his hair, forehead, and nose were rimmed with a pinkish glow from the lights of the parking lot. "One kiss, all right? I've been thinking about it ever since the shooting session, watching you all fired up behind your camera. We were sharing something together then, I thought. Something that caught both of us up and exhilarated us, excited us. Don't tell me you didn't feel it. I thought maybe that common ground was reason enough to end the night with a simple kiss."

"I told you, I'm not looking for a relationship."

"Neither am I. I'm looking for a kiss—nothing more. Because I like you, and I've enjoyed being with you and working with you, and kissing is a helluva nifty way of telling a person things like that."

There was little she could do—and in another moment, little she wanted to do—to combat him. He lowered his lips the remaining fraction of an inch, touching her mouth lightly with warm, warm lips, made all the more warm by the contrast of his cold, cold nose against the side of her face while he held her by her upper arms. Her eyes slid closed, and her guard grew shaky while the gentle pressure of his mouth lingered, growing more welcome as the seconds passed. Without removing his lips from hers, he pulled her lightly against him, guiding her resisting arms around his sides, then clamping them securely with his elbows. When he felt her stiff resistance melt, he slowly, cautiously moved his hands to her back, wrapping her up, tightening inexorably while he started things with the sensuous movement of his head—nudging, now harder, now softer, back and forth, while she felt the warm proddings of his tongue. The warning voices, reminding Allison of Jason and the hurtful past, echoed away into silence. Only the thrumming of her own heart filled her ears as her hands rested on the back of his jacket, holding him lightly. Her lips parted, and his tongue came seeking. She met the warm, wet tip with her own and felt the heart-tripping thrill of wet flesh meeting wet flesh in a first seeking dance.

Behind her she felt his hands moving brusquely and

wondered what he was doing as the motion jerked his mouth sideways on hers momentarily. The next moment she knew he'd removed a glove, for she felt his bare hand seek her warm neck, under the cascade of hair, nestling in under the twist of scarves, massaging the back of her neck and head, commanding it to tip as he willed it, holding her captive though she no longer sought escape.

Her heart hammered everywhere, everywhere as she drifted beneath his warm, wet tongue while it slid along the soft, velvet skin of her inner lips, drew circular patterns around her own before he softened the pressure of his entire mouth, nibbling at the rim of her lips, making the complete circle before widening again, the kiss now grown wholly demanding.

Their jackets were waist length. He held her around her hips with a strong arm, and she felt his body spring to life with hardness as he pressed the zipper of his blue jeans firmly against her stomach, and before she knew what she was doing, she was moving in afterbeats, making circles with her hips that chased those he made with his.

As if realizing he'd taken the kiss farther than he'd intended, Rick closed his fingers around a fistful of Allison's hair, tugging gently, gently as he dropped his head back and swallowed convulsively.

Their breaths came strident and rushed, falling in blending clouds of white as she leaned her forehead against his chin.

Rick's eyes slid closed while he bid his body to slow down.

"Wow," he got out, the word a guttural half gulp.

She chuckled, a high, tight sound of unexpectedness before two strained, little words squeezed from her throat. "Yeah . . . wow."

Her hips rested lightly against him. She waited for her body to cool down and be sensible, but against her she could feel the difficulty he, too, was having talking sense into his body.

"One kiss," he managed in a gruff voice. "That's what I promised, and I keep my promises."

Seeking to control emotions that seemed to be running away like horses with the bits between their teeth, she teased, "Would you believe I did that so convincingly just so I could get my hands on your Hasselblad?"

He laughed, raised his head, and answered, "No."

She disengaged herself from his arms, and Rick complied without further resistance.

"Well, I did," she teased, jamming her hands deep into her pockets and backing a step away. "I told you I'd sell my soul for one of them."

He smiled, his eyes on her upturned face as he drew his glove back on. "You keep that up and you might end up doing exactly that."

For a moment she had the urge to step into his embrace and try that one more time. But if she did, it might be more than his Hasselblad she wanted to get her hands on.

While she pondered, he indicated the van with an upward nudge of chin, ordering, "Get the hell in, do you hear?"

Obediently she turned and climbed aboard.

"I'll call you," he said tersely, as if trusting himself to say no more at the moment.

Then the door slammed shut, and he stepped back, feet spread wide, moving not a muscle as he watched the van back up and drive away. In the rear-view mirror she saw him as she rounded the corner. He hadn't moved from the spot.

Chapter
SEVEN

THE phone rang exactly six times the following day. Each time Allison expected to hear Rick's voice but was disappointed. Neither did he call all weekend. During the following week Allison grew more and more impatient for the sound of his voice on the other end of the line. But he didn't call.

The transparencies for the book cover came back from processing and she tried calling him but got no answer. Vivien came to see them one afternoon, gushing in her own inimitable way that the shots were *"re-e-eally nice."* Then she asked for Rick Lang's phone number.

After giving it to her, Allison wondered if Vivien called men and asked them for dates. Probably. Remembering the freewheeling kiss Vivien had laid on Rick, and the kiss she herself had shared with him, Allison couldn't say she blamed Vivien one bit.

Friday night and Saturday seemed to crawl by, and still he didn't call. Sunday morning Allison was up early and in the shower when the phone rang.

She burst from the spray stark naked and dripping, flying around the corner of the hall into the living room, skittering on the slick floor in her bare feet.

"Hello!" she exclaimed breathlessly.

"Hi." One deep-voiced syllable turned her heart into a jackhammer. "Did I wake you?"

"No. I was in the shower."

"Oh! Why don't I call you back in a few minutes?" he returned apologetically.

"No!" she almost yelped, then consciously calmed her voice. "No, it's all right." There was a puddle on the floorboards at her feet. Her breasts were covered with goose pimples, which also blossomed up and down her belly like the curried nap of a carpet. Wet hair was dripping into her eyes and streaming into her mouth. She pushed a straggly strand away from one eye as she lied, "I wasn't really in the shower. I was all done."

"Are you sure?"

"Sure I'm sure. You should see me—all bright eyed and bushy tailed." She glanced at her naked, shivering body and controlled an urge to laugh out loud.

"It's been over a week," he reminded her unnecessarily.

"Oh, has it?" Allison was shivering so badly she covered her breasts with one arm and hand, trying to keep warm.

"Very funny—*has it*," he repeated dryly, "as if I haven't been counting off every damned day."

"Then why didn't you call?"

"I was up north taking winter shots while there's still some snow left, getting last dibs in on my Hasselblad before somebody else gets her hands on it. I just got back."

"Just? You mean just now?" She checked the kitchen clock. It wasn't quite nine yet. Emily was a three-hour ride from here.

"Yes. I wanted to leave yesterday, but my mother insisted on cooking my favorites for supper last night—a convenient ruse to keep me another day, so I just pulled in."

"And?" she prompted innocently.

"And can I see you?" Beneath the hand that cupped her naked, wet breast a rush of sensuality tingled the nerve endings of her flesh. She closed her eyes and pretended it was Rick's hand.

"I have the transparencies here to sho—"

"Screw the transparencies! When can I come?"

"I have to do my—"

"When?" he demanded, then decided for her. "Never mind answering that. I'll be there in fifteen minutes."

"Fif—hey, wait!"

But it was too late. The line had gone dead. She flew back to the bathroom, stubbed her toe on the corner of the vanity, cursed volubly, and flung a towel over her hair. Frantically rubbing, she wondered which to do, hair or makeup? There wasn't time for both. Oh God, he was going to walk in here and she would look like she had just had a Baptist baptism! She flung the towel aside just as the phone rang again.

"Yes, what is it?" she demanded impatiently.

It was him again. "Have you had breakfast?"

"No."

"Well, don't!" The line went dead in her hand again, and she stared at it a moment, smiled, then flew back to the bathroom. When the doorbell rang less than twelve minutes later, she was sure it was him.

"Oh, *no-o-o!*" she wailed at her reflection in the mirror, her face sans lip gloss, blush, mascara, or even dry hair. Only one eye had pale mauve shadow above it. Like a half made-up clown she opened the door to find Rick standing on her landing hugging a grocery sack in both arms.

"Hi," he said quietly, a slow smile spreading over his face.

"Hi." A beguiling fluttering began just beneath her left breast as they stood in the cold morning air, measuring each other while the draft swirled into the apartment.

"Can I buy you breakfast?"

She couldn't seem to take in enough of him at once

144

as her eyes wandered over his face, freshly shaved and shining, while he let his gaze roam over her half made-up face.

She nodded mutely, forgetting to step back and let him in. Still holding the brown paper bag, he reached one gloved hand out and captured her neck, pulling her half outside while he leaned down to kiss her, the zigzagged edge of the crackly bag cutting into her chin. His lips were warm and impatient as his tongue slipped out to touch her surprised lips. Then he straightened, released her, and smiled sheepishly.

"Oops, I'm sorry. Here I am letting all the warm air out while your hair turns to icicles." He moved inside and glanced down her legs. She had whipped on a pair of faded jeans and a plaid cotton shirt but hadn't had a chance to put her shoes on. Self-consciously she tried to cover the bare toes of her left foot with those of her right.

His eyes moved to her wet, straight hair, and from her left eye to her right. Next he caught sight of the puddle of water on the living room floor, by the telephone.

One eyebrow lifted skeptically. "All bright eyed and bushy tailed, huh?"

"Well, sort of." She flipped her hands out only to realize she still held the brush from her eyeshadow.

The room was flooded with bright morning sunlight, cascading across the yellows and greens, dappling the gleaming hardwood floors where the plants cast leaf shadows. Rick's glance moved around, lingering longest on the puddle before returning to her face.

"Should I have waited until later to call?" he asked.

Her heart threatened to explode in her chest as she admitted, "No, I'd have gone mad waiting another hour."

The brown paper bag slid down his leg and landed on the floor with a thump. Rick's eyes devoured Allison's face while he reached out and brought her up hard against his chest, lifting her completely off the floor while he kissed her thoroughly. His tongue sought her mouth, and hers eagerly waited to meet it, moving in wild, eager greeting as if these last eight days had been agony for each of them. His teeth trapped her bottom lip, but she neither knew nor cared when she tasted the faint saltiness of blood. He fell back against the door, taking her with him, letting her body slide back down until her toes touched the floor. And in passing she realized he was hard, aroused, and marveled that she could make him so even while her hair was wet, her makeup still in its plastic cases. His hands disappeared from her back, and she began to pull away, only to be stopped.

"No, wait, don't go," he said, close to her ear, "I just want to get my gloves off so I can touch you." Behind her she heard the gloves hit the floor, then his hands pulled her close again, and she clambered right up on top of his boots with her bare feet, leaning willingly, feeling the welcome length of his body against hers. His palms slid to her buttocks to draw her harder, harder against him. She circled his neck with both arms, straining toward his lips, tongue, chest, and hips while desire flared in her. His cold palm slid beneath her shirt. When it brushed the skin just above her waistband, she flinched and shivered.

He pulled back, looking down into her eyes. "What's the matter?" His voice was deep and ragged.

"Your hands are like ice."

"Do you mind?" he asked with gruff tenderness, one cold hand already warming on her soft, willing skin.

She searched his eyes, her own gone somber, her lips fallen open, slightly swollen and glistening with moisture from his tongue.

"No." It was difficult to speak, her heartbeats were so erratic. She had missed him incredibly, found herself undeniably eager for more of his lips and hands on her. Those hands now spread wide over her ribs, which rose and fell in sharp gusts while the driving thrum of her heart seemed to lift her from his chest and drop her back against it heavily.

And then his face was lost in closeness as he kissed the side of her nose, her colored eyelid, her uncolored eyelid, her temple, and after that impossibly long wait—her mouth. He took it with tender, demanding ease, playing with her tongue, nuzzling even as he tasted, tempted, tried. His hand rode up her ribs until one

thumb rested in the hollow beneath her left breast,
where it gently stroked. Surprised when he found no
bra, he lifted his head, smiled, and murmured,
"Mmmm?"

Her arms still looped about his neck, she replied,
"Well, you only gave me ten minutes." Then she
reached to catch his upper lip between her teeth and
tugged him back where he belonged. His kiss grew ardent and searching while his hand at last filled itself
with her naked breast, its nipple puckered tight with
desire.

Into his open mouth she whispered throatily, "Rick,
what did you do to me in these last eight days?"

"Exactly what you did to me, I hope—drove me
crazy."

"But I don't want you to think I just . . . just fall
against every man who walks through that door with a
grocery bag in his arms."

"How many have walked through it that way?"

"One."

"Hell, one's not too many. Your reputation's safe."
But he backed away, grinned into her eyes, and added,
"For the time being."

And she knew her days—maybe hours—of celibacy
were numbered. She was falling for him more swiftly
than she'd fallen for Jason, and more surely, for while
she had learned to love Jason, she'd never really liked

him. But she had liked Rick Lang even before falling in love with him.

Restraining his desires, he smiled down into her eyes. "Hey, lady, did you know you have purple stuff above one eye and not the other?"

"It's mauve, not purple, and it's eyeshadow, not stuff, and I was hoping you'd be so overcome by me you wouldn't notice."

"And what about that mop of hair? You intend to leave it that way or do you want to dry it while I cook us a *real* omelette?"

"Inferring that the one I fixed us was not a real omelette?" she returned in an injured tone.

"Exactly. Mine will have ham and green pepper and onion and tomato in it, and it'll be topped with cheddar cheese."

"I can't stand green peckers," she stated tartly.

"Green *whats!*"

Immediately she colored. "Oh, Rick, I'm sorry. I . . . I . . ." She turned her back, horrified to have let the familiarity pop out unrestrained. It was an old joke between her and Jason.

"Go dry your hair. I'll holler if I can't find everything I need."

In the bathroom she glowered at her reflection in the mirror.

"Stupid twit!" she scolded her reflection.

To turn the odds in her favor, she made her bed, put on a bra, and took extra pains with her hair, styling it with the curling iron until it fluffed about her collar in wispy tendrils that bounced on her shoulders.

The sound of the stereo came to her. Smiling, Allison glanced toward the doorway, then began humming as she turned toward the mirror again.

Her makeup was subtle and iridescent, applied with a light but knowledgeable hand, for she'd made up many models in her day. As an afterthought she placed light touches of perfume behind each ear, on each wrist, then on impulse snaked a hand beneath her shirt and touched the valley between her breasts before bending to touch each ankle, too.

Straightening up, she turned to find Rick leaning indolently against the bathroom doorframe, grinning as he watched her. He let his head tip speculatively to one side while teasing, "So that's where you women put perfume, huh? I counted—there were seven places." He pulled his shoulder from the door and turned away. "Your breakfast is ready, Cleopatra."

Allison could have died on the spot.

She might have felt self-conscious meeting his eyes when she took her place at the table, but he put her at ease with his teasing. Swinging around, bearing two plates with enormous, fluffy Spanish omelettes, he unceremoniously plopped them on the table, advising, "Eat up, skinny, you look like you can use it."

"Oh, do I now? I didn't hear any complaints a few minutes ago when you came in."

"You may not have heard them, but you may recall I had a hand on your ribs, and you're about as fat as a sparrow's kneecap."

She smiled. "You sound just like my mother. Every time I go home it's, 'Allison, eat up. Allison, you just don't look healthy. Allison, have a second helping.' It drives me crazy. Why is it that mothers and grandmothers think a woman isn't healthy unless she's at least twenty pounds overweight?"

"Probably because they love you and mean the best for you. If they didn't they wouldn't bother to notice. I get the same thing from my dad when I go home, only about being single. 'Rick, you know that Benson girl moved back home and got a job in Doc Wassall's office. Didn't you used to date her when you were in high school?' " Rick grinned sardonically. "That Benson girl probably weighs a hundred and eighty now and wears support hose and orthopedic shoes. Besides, I don't think Dad would believe it if I told him I can actually cook an omelette. He's never cooked one in his life. Mom's always there to do it for him . . . *and* his laundry, his house-cleaning, and reminding him when it's time to pay the electric bill. That's their way of life. If they try to force it on me, I understand it's because they want me to be happy. So I just grin and tell Dad maybe I'll give old Ellen Marie Benson a call before I leave."

"And do you?" Allison peered up at him, suddenly curious about the women he'd dated.

"Occasionally . . . oh, not Ellen Marie, but a couple of others my folks don't know about."

"Anyone in particular?" she inquired, watching his expression carefully.

It remained noncommittal. "Nope," he answered shortly and took another mouthful of eggs.

"Speaking of calling girls, you're going to get a call from one."

"Who?" He looked up over the rim of his coffee cup.

"Vivien. She asked me for your phone number."

He chuckled. "Oh *Vivien.*" He drew out the name and followed it with a salacious grin.

Allison leaned an elbow on the table, smirking. "Do girls actually do that, I mean, call guys and . . . and boldly . . ." She stammered to a halt.

"And boldly what?"

"And boldly . . ." Allison gestured vacantly. "I don't know. What do girls boldly ask when they call guys? I've always wondered."

"Meaning you've never done it yourself?"

"Hardly. It's not my style."

His eyes danced over her pink cheeks, and he leaned his elbows on either side of his plate, a coffee cup in one hand. "I'm glad."

"You are?" Her eyes were wide and innocent now, meeting his over the cup.

"Yes, I am. Because I'm one of those guys who still wants to do the pursuing as if women's lib never came along and gave women the idea of doing it themselves."

"Judging from the kiss Vivien treated you to, I'd say you're in for some mighty diligent pursuing from that quarter."

He lifted his chin and laughed lightly, leaning back in his chair. "Oh, that Vivien, she's incorrigible." Yet he didn't fawn over the fact. Instead he made light of it, suffering no bloated ego, which pleased Allison. All of a sudden the corners of his mouth drifted down into a placid expression as he studied her. His eyes moved over her hair, ears, mouth, cheeks, and came at last to her wide brown eyes. "Your hair is very pretty," he said quietly.

A stab of warmth flooded her cheeks, and her eyelids fluttered down momentarily. He crossed his hands over his stomach and continued studying her pink, flustered cheeks and the self-conscious way her eyes cast about for something to settle on. They came to rest on his knuckles. "And so is the rest of you," he added.

A warning signal went off in her head. Was this his line? It was different from Jason's, which never included compliments quite this simple, but rather effusive hosannas on how she "turned him on." Remembering them now, Allison told herself to slow down, beware, things were going too fast.

But she experienced a heady feeling of pleasure in

being the object of his admiring scrutiny as he leaned back in his chair with casual ease, his voice coming softly again. "You have butter on your top lip." Her hand reacted self-consciously, grabbing the paper napkin from her lap and lifting it toward her mouth. Halfway there, his came out to stop it. He leaned across the corner of the table while her eyes flew up in alarm.

"Would you mind very much if I kissed it off?"

His eyes remained steady on Allison while her throat muscles shifted as she swallowed. Her brown gaze held a startled expression. Her lips fell open in surprise while she sat as still as a bird in deep camouflage, staring back at Rick.

"Would you?" he repeated so softly it was nearly a murmur.

Her wariness fled, chased away by his soft, persuasive question. The negative movement of her head was almost imperceptible. Eyes locked with hers, Rick removed the napkin from her numb fingers, crossed her palm with his, in the fashion of an Indian handshake, only gently, as if he held a crushable flower. As he leaned by degrees across the corner of the table, the pressure of his fingers increased, and he brought the back of her hand firmly against his chest. She felt the heavy thud of his heart as his eyes slid closed, and his lips touched her buttery upper lip, lightly sucking, licking, moving across its width from corner to corner before he did the same to her bottom lip. Allison felt as if melting butter were rippling down the center of her stomach, ending in a fluttering delight between her legs.

He backed away a fraction of an inch so that only the tip of his tongue circled her mouth, which eased more fully open until her own tongue did his bidding, just its tip caressing the tip of his while beneath her hand the hammering of his heart grew almost violent.

He took his long, sweet time at it, tempting her with unhurried leisure, backing away an inch that made her eyes drift open to find his had done the same. He rested his forehead against hers, nudging softly, then backing away again so they could gaze into each other's eyes. His calculated slowness caused an insistent throbbing within the deep reaches of Allison's body. His eyes stayed on hers while he gradually brought her hand between their two mouths, opening his lips in slow motion, taking her thumb gently between his teeth, making miniature, caressing motions of gnawing, while his chin moved left and right, left and right, and his eyes burned into hers. He moved on to her index finger, biting its knuckle before straightening it with a flick of his thumb. She watched, fascinated and sensualized as it disappeared into the warm, wet confines of his mouth.

The gushing responses in her body were like nothing Jason had ever elicited from her, short of climaxes, which he had carefully regulated and often delighted in denying until she begged. Now, as Allison's finger was caressed by Rick's tongue, her body felt ready to explode. Gradually he slipped the finger from his mouth, then turned her hand over and gently bit its outer edge, his eyelashes drifting down to create a fan of shadow on his cheek while his labored breathing told her what this foreplay was doing to him, too.

He fell utterly still for a long, long moment, resting the backs of her fingertips against his lips, eyes closed as if in deep meditation. When he lifted his lids to study her, he spoke hoarsely, with her knuckles still touching his lips, muffling the words. "I didn't think I'd make it through these last eight days. You don't know how many times I went to the phone and stood there staring at it, wanting to call. But I remembered what you said about not wanting a relationship, and I was sure you'd say you didn't want to see me again."

His words sent a wild reverberation of joy through Allison.

"Are you for real?" she managed at last, letting her eyes travel over what she could see of his face behind their hands. "I mean, look at yourself. Look at your face and your . . . your form, and tell me why you should be worried about whether or not one girl wanted to see you again."

"Is that all you see when you look at me? A face and a . . . a form?" he queried.

"No." She swallowed, retrieved her hand, and picked up her coffee cup to have a reason for withdrawing from him. "But why me?"

"If you don't know, if you can't feel it, I can't explain. I thought what was just happening here a moment ago was explanation enough—that, along with some enjoyable hours we've spent together."

"Rick . . . I . . ." She quickly rose to her feet, taking their plates to the sink so she could turn her back on him. She heard his chair scrape back and knew he was standing directly behind her.

"You don't trust me, do you? You think I'm handing you a practiced line of bull."

"Something like that," she admitted. In her entire life no man had ever so effectively seduced her as he'd just done across the corner of a breakfast table, touching no more than her hand. He had to know his appeal—all he had to do was look in the mirror to see he was no Hunchback of Notre Dame. And he had a wooing, winning way that could easily turn a woman's head.

"You want me to act like an admiring monk, is that it?"

She rested the palms of her hands against the edge of the sink, staring straight ahead, not knowing what she wanted, afraid of things her body was compelling her to do.

"I don't know," she choked, near tears, so confused by her impulses to trust him, those impulses juxtaposed against past experiences that had always turned out disastrously when she too eagerly placed her trust in another person.

A heavy hand fell on the side of her neck, kneading

lightly. "I'm sorry, Allison. I promised, didn't I?" Even the touch he bestowed so casually made her heart race. Silence ticked by for several seconds, then Rick said quietly, "But after what happened at the door when I came in, I thought—"

"My mistake, letting it happen, okay?" she quickly interjected, afraid to turn around and face him. "I *was* glad to see you, and you just caught me a little off guard, that's all."

"You feel you have to erect a guard against me, is that what you're saying?"

"I . . . yes," she admitted.

"Why?"

She refused to answer. His warm hand lowered to the center of her back and began stroking up and down. "I'm not him, Allison," he said in the gentlest tone imaginable.

The hair at the back of her neck bristled. Her shoulder blades tensed. "Who?" she snapped.

"I don't know. You tell me." His hands circled her upper arms and forced her to turn around.

"I don't know what you're talking about," she lied, staring at the floor.

"Neither do I. What was his name?"

Her lips compressed into a thin line. He watched her face for every nuance of truth while dropping his hands from her. He stepped back, crossing his arms, then his calves, leaning his hips against the edge of the kitchen stove behind him.

"Do you want to tell me about him?"

"Him! Him!" she spouted belligerently. "You don't know what you're talking about."

"The man who made you so defensive and jumpy and wary of me, that's who I'm talking about. What was his name?"

"There is no such man!"

"Bull!" he returned tightly.

Her eyes met his determinedly. *"There is no man in my life,"* she stated unequivocally.

"No, but there was, wasn't there?"

"It's none of your business."

"Like hell it isn't. If he's what's keeping you from me, it's my business."

"I'm what's keeping me from you! I'm cautious, all right? Is there any crime in that?" she shouted in a sudden display of hot temper.

Rick scowled, studying her with a hard expression about his mouth. "Boy, he soured you on men but good, didn't he? Made up your mind you'll never trust one of us again, is that it?"

"Trust is another thing that never profited me one damn bit in the end," she stated bitterly.

"And so you're done with it, no matter what your gut feeling tells you?"

She suddenly bristled, gesturing angrily with her hands in the air, storming away. "I don't have to stand here for this . . . this third degree! This is my house, and

159

just because I let you come in and cook breakfast for me doesn't give you the right to assess my motives. I thought of you, too, during the last week." She swung around to face him. "Is that what you want to hear? All right, I did! And I knew before the second day was gone that I wanted to see you again. But don't probe into my past if you want to share any of my future, be it a day, a week, or a month, because I won't stand for it!" She was back before him, practically nose to nose, bristling with defensiveness, striking out at him because she was afraid of the overwhelming urges she felt to like him, to trust him, maybe even to fall in love with him.

He stared at her angrily for a moment, and she saw his eyebrows finally relax from their tightly knit curl, his mouth take on a less pinched expression as he made a conscious effort to quell the urge to argue.

"You're right. It's none of my business," he agreed, backing off, shelving the issue for the time being. "Peace offering, all right?"

He pulled away from the stove and dipped a hand into the brown paper bag that was still on top of the counter. The next moment he lifted a camera in a black leather case. He held it aloft in invitation, its wide, woven strap swinging in the sudden silence between them.

Her animosity fell away with amusing speed, to be replaced by excited surprise. "The . . . the Hasselblad?" she asked breathlessly.

"The Hasselblad."

She reached for it, but he pulled it back just beyond her fingertips. "Wait a minute. Aren't you the woman who said you'd sell your soul for a chance to use it?"

Here it comes, Allison thought, the proposition.

But he only grinned one-sidedly, leaning over from the hip to place his mouth within easy kissing distance. "I won't ask for your soul, just one little kiss to bring peace back between us."

She gave him the price he asked, a quick, fleeting smack, but he still refused to give her the camera. "Friends?" he inquired, grinning into her face.

"Friends," she agreed, and snatched the camera from his hand.

Behind her she heard a throaty chuckle as she whirled toward the sunny living room to sit cross-legged on the shag rug. He ambled over and joined her, sitting almost knee to knee with her. He produced a roll of film and smiled, watching as she loaded the camera, exhilarated now, all attention given over to the coveted piece of equipment.

"Here's the film advance." He pointed to a silver crank. "And here's the shutter release." Her face was a picture of radiance as she looked down into the magnified square to study the light falling through the long, narrow windows. She spun around on her derrière, then rolled to her knees, walking on them across the hardwood floor while scanning the room through the viewfinder, looking for a setting that caught her eye.

The camera fell against her tummy. "Over there!" she ordered, pointing.

"Where? What?" He played dumb.

She wagged a finger at the floor to an oblique square of morning sun. "Over there, quick! Just sit the way you are, only do it over there, and face the kitchen so your face is sidelit."

He complied, smiling, sitting on the floor in the warm wash of sunlight, drawing his knees up, crossing his arms loosely over them. Allison lay on the floor before him, flat on her belly with her elbows braced on the floor, directing the tilt of his head in this direction and that. The natural window light illuminated the side of his face, put highlights on one side of his thick hair, lit the top of an ear, and left a solid line of shadow beyond the ridge of his forehead, nose, lips, and chin. She took two shots, then popped up, dragged a schefflera plant across two feet of floor, and ordered, "Now, with the shadows of the leaves on your face . . . but no smiles, okay? Turn a little more toward the window and give me that handsome seriousness and let the mouth speak of thoughtfulness." The shutter clicked two more times, and her exuberant face appeared above the Hasselblad, a puckish smile on her mouth. "You're stunning, Rick Lang, do you know that?"

The camera freed her and let her natural impulses bubble out. With it around her neck, she felt totally uninhibited, released to speak what she felt. Only without the camera was she thwarted by the idea of getting involved with personal emotions.

"How about the basket chair?" he suggested next.

"Ahhh, perfect. Get in."

He pushed himself up off the floor and plopped onto the cushioned seat while she directed the chair opening toward the light source with an acute instinct for shadow effect and camera angle. She peered down into the viewfinder, checked the composition, lowered the camera, and looked around. She bounced across the room to drag a potted palm over, knelt down, and framed the shot with a spiky frond, making sounds of delight deep in her throat when she found the composition to her liking.

When she'd satisfied her artist's eye at that setting, she scanned the room, pointed to the French doors leading to the porch, and asked if he'd mind going out there where it was cold.

"What'll you give me?" he teased. "I work by the hour, you know."

She plopped a passing kiss on his mouth, hardly conscious of what she was doing, so caught up was she with the joy of photographing with the prized piece of equipment.

She framed him through the panes of the French door, adjusting the angle of the camera time and again in an attempt to create a well-composed photo without hiding his features behind the crossbars of the window frames.

"Hey, hurry up!" he complained, his voice coming muffled through the closed door. "My nipples are puckering up."

She laughed, snapped two quick ones, told him he could come back in, then admitted, "Mine, too," adding impudently, "they always do when I get turned on, and your camera really turns me on."

"Only my camera, huh?"

"I didn't say that, did I?"

"Well, let me know when you want to indulge in a little puckering. Maybe we can work together on it, without the help of porch or camera."

When she'd exhausted all the best possibilities the apartment offered for settings, she was still rarin' to go. "How about doing some outside shots?" he suggested. "There's a Winterfest going on at Lake Calhoun this afternoon, and I was planning to ask if you wanted to go over and fool around anyway."

"Fool around?" she repeated archly.

"With the camera, of course," he returned. "There's all kinds of stuff going on over there. What do you say we bundle up warm and check it out?"

He was irresistible, and she *did* want a chance to get to know him better. And she *did* want to work with the camera a little longer. And she *did* so enjoy being with him.

"Why not?" Allison replied, jubilant at the thought of spending a whole afternoon with him without having to talk her emotions into a state of equilibrium because privacy offered him a chance to kiss or touch her.

Chapter
EIGHT

S HE donned her disreputable bobcap and scarf,
and thigh-high boots lined with fur and a hip-
length jacket belted at the waist. From the trunk
of his car Rick dug out an enormous parka. He let the
hood flop down his back, but the wolf-fur lining, fram-
ing his chin and jaw, set off his masculinity to great advantage. Even before they got in the car, Allison
snapped a shot of him, having adjusted the f-stop to
compensate for the blinding brightness of the snow
outside.

It was a dazzling day, as bright as their spirits as they
drove the short distance to Lake Calhoun. The Winterfest was already in full swing when they arrived, the ac-

tivities taking place right on the frozen lake, which looked like a confetti blanket, its white surface dotted with multicolored wool caps and bright ski jackets. Wandering from event to event, Allison snapped random shots—two runny-nosed eight-year-olds angling for sunfish through a hole in the ice; the laughing face of a man who'd fallen onto his back like an overturned turtle during a game of broomball; a young married couple sculpturing an ice mermaid by wetting down snow and compacting it with mittens covered with plastic bags; a string of red-nosed youngsters at the finish line of an ice-skating race, their lips set in grim determination; a boy and girl kissing, unaware that Allison was snapping them because their eyes were closed; an ice boat with its orange-and-yellow sail furled by the breeze, its rider hanging over the edge at a precarious angle; Rick lying flat on his back, making an angel in the snow; the grand, old Calhoun Beach Hotel Building—which was a hotel no longer—standing across the road from the lake in majestic watchfulness while funseekers romped and played and totally disregarded the fact that the temperature was only twelve degrees above zero.

Rick brought hot chocolate from a stand that had also been on the ice. They sat on a snowbank, squinting through the steam rising from their cups, watching a judge measuring a ridiculously short pickerel with a tape measure while a small boy looked on hopefully. Allison felt Rick's eyes on her instead of on the fishing contest, and turned to meet his gaze.

"You're the neatest girl I ever met, you know that?"

Flustered, she looked away and hid behind a sip of cocoa.

"Don't hide, it's nothing to be ashamed of. You're game for anything—bundling up and clumping out here in this cold, taking pictures of stuff that to some would seem so ridiculously bourgeois they'd scoff at the suggestion of even coming here, much less recording the homey events on film."

"It's been fun," she replied honestly, then braved a look into his eyes, adding, "and I've had a wonderful day."

"Me too."

For a moment she thought he was going to kiss her. With her heart already fluttering greedily in her throat, she suddenly didn't trust her own common sense, so she put on a pained expression and informed him, "But my derrière is so damn cold there's no feeling left in it."

Abruptly he laughed. "How 'bout your nipples?" he teased secretively. "Anything happening to them?"

"None of your business, you dirty old lech."

He licked his lips, gave her a suggestive head-to-toe scan, and grinned. "Like hell it isn't."

She hauled herself to her feet and reached out a mittened hand to give him a tug. When he was on his feet, Rick bracketed her temples with gloved hands. Her heart went a-thudding in anticipation, but he only pushed her drooping bobcap up out of her eyes and teased, "Nice cap, Scott." Then he kissed the end of her icy nose, bundled her up against his side, and hauled her with him, pressed hip to hip while they walked to the car.

Pulling up in her driveway sometime later, she moved a hand toward the door handle. His glove crossed over her arm. "Wait," he commanded.

She listened to his footsteps crunch around the rear of the car, and a moment later her door was opened. She had to giggle at his gallantry when she was dressed in her urchin's outfit, totally unflattering and unfeminine.

He followed close behind her as they climbed the stairs in slow motion. At the landing, when she aimed the key for the lock, he took it from her hand and opened the door for her, then dropped the key into her mitten. He looked into her eyes and once more pressed his palms to the sides of her head and pushed the bobcap back where it was supposed to be. But he left his hands on her cheeks this time and said into her eyes, "I want to come in."

Her lips opened to say no, it was dangerous, their feelings were rioting too fast, they needed time to assess what was happening. But before she could speak he slowly lowered his mouth to hers and her heart fluttered to life and sent quivers to her breasts. As the kiss lingered, he released her face, taking her in his arms to pull her against his bulky jacket.

She pressed her mittened hands against his back, drawing close and moving her mouth languorously beneath his, opening her lips to invite his seeking tongue. It was hot, wet, tantalizing, seductive, and it stroked away the memory of Jason. His hands roved down the back of her jacket, then underneath it. Spreading his hands wide, he gathered her close against him, spanning her icy buttocks with warm, wide palms.

His lips left her mouth. He bent his face into the warm hair at her neck, burrowing deep to find skin inside the folds of scarf. "Allison," he murmured gruffly, "let me come in. I want to warm you up."

You already have, she thought, delighting in the feel of his palms against that intimate part of her body. He drew back, deliberately lifting first the hem of his parka, then her jacket, recapturing her buttocks to pull her against the long ridge of flesh inside his jeans, to let it speak for him as he pressed its heat against her stomach. He undulated his hips, grinding against her while on her backside his hands asserted themselves and controlled her.

He kissed her with a wild thrusting of tongues, rhythmically matching the strokes of tongue and hip before jerking his mouth aside and begging in a raspy voice, "Let me come in, Allison."

She knew what he was asking and was abashed to find she wanted to do his bidding, to invite him not only into her house, but into her body as well. But she pressed her hands against his chest, begging, "Please, Rick, please stop. It's too soon, too sudden."

"What are you afraid of?" he asked.

She swallowed, reached for his hands, and brought them between them, folding his palms between her own while looking deeply into his eyes.

"Me," she admitted.

He drew in a deep, shuddering breath, put a few more inches between their bodies, and asked, "So you'd turn a man away hungry?"

"Is it supper you want?" She knew it wasn't, not any more than it was what she wanted.

"I guess I'll have to settle for it, if that's the only way I can stay."

It seemed a reprieve. She wanted him with her yet, and supper was a plausible excuse to keep him a while longer.

"I have a pizza in the freezer. How does that sound?"

"Like a hell of a poor second, but I accept."

They moved inside, but when the door was closed and the lights snapped on, there was no denying that the sexual tension remained, as vibrant as before. She hung up their jackets and turned from the pursuit in his eyes, telling her heart to calm down. But it felt deliciously good, this business of being pursued. It was beginning to dawn on her why Jason Ederlie had eaten it up so.

Allison was halfway across the living room when she was swung around abruptly by an elbow. "What's the hurry?" he teased, swinging her against him, holding her loosely around the waist, leaning back so their hips touched.

"Are you about to extract payment for the use of your Hasselblad?" she asked, resting her hands on his inner elbows, striving to keep the mood light.

"Not at all. You can keep it awhile . . . unconditionally."

"God, how can you let a camera like that lay around in its case all the time, then lend it out to some girl who . . . who . . ."

"Puckers up at the sight of it?" he finished. "Well, if you can't make the girl pucker up at the sight of you, you do the next best thing, right?" His hand wandered to her breast to brush it testingly with the backs of his fingers.

"Rick, stop it. You came in here for pizza."

"Did I?" But the humor fell from his face as he reached to take the back of her head with both hands and pull her hard against his mouth. She forgot caution and flung her arms around his neck, a hand twining into the thick hair above his collar as he made sounds of frustrated passion deep in his throat. Stars and suns and moons seemed to flash across the darkness behind Allison's closed eyelids while she let her tongue and hips and hands respond to the plea in his eyes. He tore his lips from hers. They buried their faces in each other's necks, clinging, learning the scent of each other, the texture of skin, of hair, of clothing as his hands played over her hips, and hers over the taut muscles of his shoulders and back.

"Allison, this afternoon seemed like a year," he ground out, his voice gone low. His hand cupped the back of her head, losing itself in her hair. "I swear, woman, I don't know what's happening to me."

In an effort to control the body that threatened to burst its skin, she laughed—a throaty, deep sound that came out very shaky. "I think it's called hunger pains. Let me put the pizza in."

Reluctantly he released her, his eyes darkly following the sway of her narrow hips while she crossed to the kitchen, turned on the oven, and opened the freezer door. He turned away, unable to watch her and retain control. He ambled to the component set and switched on the radio, wandered aimlessly about the living room to find himself once again drawn near the kitchen, his eyes riveted to her backside while she leaned over to slip the pizza into the oven. The back of her jeans was faded to a paler blue in twin patches just below the pockets. His eyes roved over them and he inhaled a deep, shaky breath before letting his eyelids slide closed. He ran a palm down the zipper of his jeans and pressed it hard against his tumescence.

When he opened his eyes again, she was facing him. Her cheeks lit up to a fiery red, and she bit her bottom lip, then swallowed hard.

"It's no secret," he admitted gruffly, "so why pretend? I've spent the entire afternoon thinking about one handful of warm breast in the early morning when I came here today, and somehow it just hasn't been enough."

She backed up against the oven door, reaching behind her to grab the handle in both hands to steady herself. Her face was a mask of uncertainty, and her breath fell hard and heavy from her chest.

"Rick, I'm no virgin," she admitted, abashed, yet facing him squarely.

"Neither am I. So what?"

"I'm a woman, and we're the ones who have been taught since puberty that it's up to us to control situations like this. But I feel like I'm losing control, and I don't want you to think I'm easy." She suddenly covered her face with both hands and spun around, afraid to face the hour of reckoning she knew was at hand.

How long did she think she could play with fire? How long did she think she could string along a healthy, virile, and willing twenty-five-year-old man? And what was she going to do now that she'd backed herself into this corner?

"Rick, you were right, I'm scared."

"Of what?" he asked, close behind her. "Of me?" His hand touched her hair, smoothing it gently, without the slightest hint of force. "Allison, look at me . . . please. Don't hide from it. It's nothing to be scared of."

She turned at the gentle pressure of his fingers on her neck and lifted quavering eyes to his. A moment later her voice came, shaky, unsure, doubtful. "I don't think I like being a woman in this . . . this liberated age," she admitted. "I'm not very good at being a . . . a casual lay."

His hands bracketed her jaw, lifting her face so he could look deeply into her eyes. A thumb stroked the hollow of her cheek. "Thank God," he said softly.

She lunged against him, turning her cheek upon his chest, squeezing her eyes shut, wrapping her arms tightly about his sides. "Oh, Rick, what happened to the days when a man and woman went to the altar as virgins and learned about each other in their wedding bed and stayed in it for seventy-five years, forsaking all others? That's what I'm afraid of . . . It's not there anymore!"

She could hear the steady thrum of his heart beneath her ear, then the deep rumble of his voice as he spoke reassuringly. "Allison, I don't care if there's been someone else. It doesn't change how I feel about you. What you are now you wouldn't be if you hadn't lived your life as you have so far. Does that make any sense?"

"Nothing makes any sense when I'm near you. I try to think clearly, but everything goes blurry. The only time things aren't blurry is when I'm behind the camera. Then things are clear, uncomplicated, I can understand them. If I could . . . could turn a focus ring on my life and bring it into focus as easily as I can a picture, I'd feel I had control of my life."

"And if you let your defenses down with me, your life goes out of control?"

"Yes!" She pulled back, looking up at him with haunted eyes. "Don't you see? It's like turning it all over to you. That's what scares me."

"I don't want to control your life, Allison. I want to make love to you." Gently he drew her near, raising her chin while he spoke.

She studied him, wanting to believe but afraid to. "They're both the same thing," she said shakily.

"Not with the right person."

He kissed her left eyelid closed, then her right.

"Don't," she breathed.

As if she hadn't spoken, he wrapped his arms around her, pinning her arms to her sides in the strong circle of his own. He leaned to kiss her neck. Her eyelids remained closed as she dropped her head to the side.

"Don't," she whispered raggedly.

But his lips moved to hers while he held her with one arm, peering past her cheek as he turned off the oven. Continuing to control her movements with his own, he opened the oven door while pulling her two steps away to make room for its downward swing.

"Don't."

Keeping his arm around her, he leaned to pick up a potholder from the top of the stove, then bent her over half backwards, half sideways, while he got the pizza out of the oven and set it on a burner.

The heat on the backs of her legs was nothing compared to that springing through her body as she repeated weakly, "Don't."

He manipulated her at will, dipping to reach the oven door and close it again before marching her slowly backwards in his arms across the kitchen, kissing her all the way. He stopped to turn off the dining room light, but didn't stop kissing, only opened his eyes and peered across her nose to find the light switch and snap it down while she mumbled with her lips pressed against his, "Don't."

He danced her backwards with slow, deliberate pushes of his thighs against hers, kissing her now open mouth as they progressed across the dining area toward the living room. He released her arms, found them with his hands, and forced them up over his shoulders, still walking her inexorably backwards while her body tingled and strained against him with each step.

At the stereo he dipped again, punched a button, then let his eyelids drift closed, kissing her while his tongue delved deep into her mouth, all the while idly playing the radio dial across the scanner until he'd found something soft and vocal with a guitar background. Her arms were now looped around his neck without resistance, and her words were nearly unrecognizable, spoken as they were with her tongue pressed flat against his: "Don't . . . waste . . . so . . . much . . . time."

He smiled, devouring her mouth while his hands slid down to her buttocks, pressing their shifting muscles as he hauled her step by agonizingly slow step to the light switch by the entry door. After he'd fumbled for it behind her back, his hand returned to her buttocks. He held her firmly against him in the dark until neither of them seemed able to strain close enough against the other. His thighs pushed against hers again, and she took a faltering step back to feel something solid against her shoulder blades. Wedged between his warm flesh and the wall, her breath came in onslaughts as he pressed his hips against hers, moving in sensual circles until she responded, beginning to move, too. Her shirt went sliding out of her jeans as he pulled it up with both hands, easing away from her with all but his mouth, which continued plundering in welcome attack. Behind his neck she unbuttoned her cuffs. He sensed what she was doing, stopped kissing her, and leaned his forearms on the wall beside her head.

"Unbutton the rest of it for me," he begged, his voice gravelly with emotion while his breath whisked her lips. With scarcely a pause, her trembling fingers moved to the top button. He leaned his head low in the dark, feeling with his mouth to see if she was doing as he asked. When the first button was free, his lips pressed warmly against the skin inside, above the bra. She hesitated, lost in delight as the touch of his tongue fell on her flesh. Then, keeping his palms pressed flat on the wall, he bent his head even lower, nudging her fingers to the next button, which opened at his wordless command. This time when he pressed his lips inside he met the small embroidered flower at the center of her bra. He breathed outward gently, warming her skin beneath the garment, sending shivers of desire to the peaks of her breasts. When at last her blouse hung completely open, he ordered in a husky whisper, "Now mine," hovering so close his breath left warm, damp dew on her nose.

She reached out in the dark, exploring the front-button band of his shirt running down its length. When her hand reached the waistband of his jeans he sucked in a hard, quick breath and jerked slightly. With both hands she explored his hips, just above the tight cinch of waistband. He was hard, honed, not a ripple of flesh that shouldn't be there. When her hands reached the hollow of his spine, she slowly tugged his shirttails out.

"Allison." His voice was thick and throaty. "How I've wished for this."

"And how I wanted to wish, but I was afraid."

"Are you always this slow?" came his gruff question at her cheek, and in the dark she smiled.

"Mmm-hmm, I like it slow."

"Me too, but I can't wait any long . . ." The last word was swallowed up by her mouth as his came against it while he speedily loosened his remaining buttons.

He laid his warm hand inside the open neck of her shirt, caressing her throat before pushing the garment back from her shoulders to fall to the floor behind her. His arms slid around her ribs, fingers testing their way to the clasp of her bra. It came away in his hands, leaving her half naked, eager for the caress of his palm upon her bare flesh. He stepped back, taking the bra down her arms, and in the dark she heard a rustle as he tucked it into his hind pocket. She waited, breath caught in her throat, for the return of his touch, expecting a warm cupping of her breast.

But he, too, seemed to be hovering in wait.

She reached out a tentative hand, seeking texture, seeking warmth, remembering the look of him standing in the studio, straight, erect, with his shirt off, while she assessed his almost square chest muscles studded with lightly strewn hair as pale in color as a glass of champagne, the light refracting off them as if caught in champagne bubbles.

Her hands now found what they sought, sensitive fingertips fanning across the hard muscles, the soft hair, the firm skin that shuddered beneath her touch, surprising her.

"Richard Lang," she murmured, almost as if to remind herself she was here, that it was he whose skin had just reacted so sensuously to her touch.

An almost pained sound came raspily from his throat while he scooped her against him, coaxing her bare breasts to his half-exposed chest. His lips and tongue swooped down again, working their magic as he pulled her away from the wall and took her with him, this time stepping backwards himself, feeling her legs brush his as she followed his lead.

In front of the stereo he stopped, studying her face by the dim light radiating from the face of the dial. Scant though it was, Allison could make out the outline of his features, the points of light caught in his eyes as he wrestled his shirt off, then draped it across the top of the closed turntable. He stood away from Allison, reaching first to touch her eyebrows while her lids lowered and a shudder possessed her body. His fingertips trailed over her cheeks, touched her lips, then after what seemed an eternity, found her waiting breasts.

She opened her eyes languorously. His were cast down, watching his hands. She, too, followed his glance to witness long fingers gently adoring, caressing, exploring, while beside them a voice sang, "It was easy to love her, easier than whiling away a summer's day . . ."

He touched her with tentative reserve, almost a reverence, until she could stand it no longer and covered the backs of his hands with her own, pulling his palms full and hard against her, twisting repeatedly at the waist to abrade his palms with the side to side brushing of her nipples, all hard and eager and tightened into little knots of desire.

"Allison . . ." he uttered, and dropped to one knee, reaching his mouth up to cover the hardened peak with his lips and suckle it with his tongue. "You're beautiful."

She felt beautiful as his words washed over her and a strong forearm pulled her hips against the fullest part of his chest. Her head fell back weakly, a soft sound of abandon issuing from her throat while she undulated slowly against him, brushing, brushing, with light strokes that moved her in sensual rhythm. She ran languid fingers through his hair, lost in sensation, while he moved his mouth to her other breast and took its nipple gently between his teeth, tugging lightly before circling it with his tongue, sending shivers of desire coursing through her body.

The song on the radio changed, and as if to verify the softly uttered confidences of minutes ago, a feminine voice crooned about wanting a man with a slow hand.

And a slow hand it was, slow and sensual and arousing Allison's passions until her breathing grew labored and her limbs felt as if she were moving against swift water.

Rick was on his feet again, moving against her in the age-old language of rhythm and thrust, compelling her hips to seek a mate. He backed away, guiding Allison to the soft cushions of the wicker sofa, leading her by a wrist, then urging her down with the gentle pressure of his hands on her shoulders until she lay on her back while he knelt on the floor beside her.

A strong hand found the hollow beneath her jaw, while his other one slipped behind her head, controlling the kiss that moved from mouth to nose to eyes, questing, testing. When Rick's mouth found hers again, his tongue slipped within, riding against hers in rhythm to the music, the song's sensual words underlining their feelings about this act they were sharing.

While his left hand remained buried in her hair, his right traveled down the center of her bare stomach, following the zipper of her jeans until he cupped the warmth between her legs, pressing, pressing, unable to press hard enough to satisfy either of them, exploring through tight, restrictive denim until she raised one knee and her hips jutted up, bringing her body hard and thrusting against his touch.

Lowering his mouth to her breast, he continued his exploration, pressing the heel of his hand against the mound of flesh hidden yet from him, delighting in her response as small sounds of passion came from her throat, and she strained upward with arousal and the need for more. He kissed the hollow between her ribs, burying his face in the wider hollow just above her waistband, feeling the driving beats of her breath as her stomach lifted his face time and again.

He raised his head. With one tug, the snap of her jeans gave, and she fell utterly still, not breathing, not moving, but waiting . . . waiting. The rasp of the zipper seemed to match the sound of Rick's strident breathing.

When his palm slipped inside, against her stomach, pent-up breath fell from Allison in a wild rush, and she flung one arm above her head while wholly giving over the control of her body to him. His hand slid lower, fingers delving inside brief, silken bikinis until they brushed flattened hair and moved beyond, contouring her flesh, seeking, finding, sliding within the warm wet confines of her femininity. Her ribs arched high off the cushions as he began a slow, rhythmic stroking to which her body answered.

She lowered the arm from above her head, seeking to

know him in the dark, then rolled slightly toward him and found his hot, hard body, while he knelt with knees spread wide, ready. He made a guttural sound deep in his throat, and she caressed him more boldly, learning the shape of him through his jeans. He leaned to nuzzle her neck, and as his nipple touched hers she could feel the torturous hammering of his heart against her own.

The moments that followed were a rapturous swirl of sensation as they pleasured each other with touches. There no longer seemed a need for lips to join. Only their cheeks rested lightly against each other while they savored this bodily prelude and honed their senses to a fine edge.

He was so different from Jason, unrushed and sensitive to her every need. "You like that?" he whispered against her breast, laughing deep in his throat when she answered, "Yes, do it again." He washed the entire orb of her breast with his tongue again, wetting all of its surface until shivers radiated across the aroused skin.

He slid his lips to the corner of her mouth. "Lift up," he whispered, hands at her hips. And in the next moment, both denim and satin were down around her hips, then gone, whispered away from her ankles. His hands deserted her body, and she listened to the rustle, snap, and zip as he freed himself in like manner, found her hand, and once again led it to him.

He leaned over, burying his face in the warm hollow of her waistline as a shudder overcame him and he held her wrist, guiding her to stroke his velvet sleekness. Then they were lost in each other, in the moving, touching, and trembling. They reveled in the taking and giving of sensory delights while the darkness whispered their intimacies. Time had no limits as they explored with slow ease, thrilling to the realization that they had found each other. Somehow, in this wide world of countless souls, theirs had managed to meet and strike a chord of kindred need and compatibility.

They felt rich and blessed, at times awed that they should be this lucky. They were, in those minutes, open and unencumbered, hiding neither the passion to give nor the pleasure in taking, extending the anticipation of the final blending until their bodies writhed and burned.

But soon the heat and height grew too great for Rick. "Allison, stop . . . stop . . ." He grabbed her wrist and pinned it above her head, pulled in a deep, shuddering breath and lay his hips just beside hers. "I'm outdistancing you, darling," he whispered thickly, "but there's no hurry, we have all night." He kissed her eyelid, the side of her nose, continuing his silken arousal of her even while temporarily denying himself fulfillment. Again his mouth was at her breast, teeth, tongue, and lips sending ripples of impatience radiating everywhere. The tumult he'd started rumbled close to the surface—higher, higher, until Allison's head arched back, her body now moving to meet his velvet touches. Through clenched teeth she whispered a single word, "Please . . ." knowing he would stop, leaving her at the brink of that hellish heaven where her body would be exposed in its most vulnerable state.

But it was Rick, not Jason, who wielded the touch of fire in which she burned. And rather than withdraw it, he extended it as Allison had never known it could be extended, until her muscles went taut and the goodness lengthened and strengthened and took her tumbling into the world of sensation as her body became a choreographed dance of muscle and motion.

In the height of her passion, Allison's palms unknowingly pressed his mouth away from her nipples, which had suddenly gone sensitive while she shuddered and cried out in a half sob, half laugh.

When she drifted down to earth from the place of lush quickening, his hand was stroking her languid legs, his kiss etching its mark upon her damp stomach. Weakly she reached to lift his face back to hers. "I didn't mean to push you away. I'm sorry . . ."

His kiss cut off her apology. "For what?" came his throaty whisper. "Allison, that was beautiful. I never thought you'd be so . . . so free and open with me." He kissed her neck, his voice a loud rumble in her ear as a hand ran from her knees to her waist and back again. "God, Allison, that was more than beautiful. It was an accolade."

"It was selfish," she insisted, abashed at her total abandon.

"No . . . no," he assured her against her lips.

"But I forgot all about you in the middle of it." She lay a palm along his cheek and felt him smile as he chuckled.

"But I'm next, darling."

She rolled to her side, brushed her hand down his stomach to find him taut, silken, waiting. The next moment, she felt herself being tugged into a sitting position, insistent hands stroking her spine and urging her toward the edge of the cushions. He leaned away. Warm touches guided her to do his bidding. Her knee brushed his hard stomach as he parted her knees and settled himself between them. "Come here," came his voice thickly. Then he pulled her hard and tight against him and tilted her back with a gentle pressure of his palm upon her chest. There came a rustle in the dark, and she felt a cushion fill the void between her back and the sofa. His hands found her hips, moved sleekly down the backs of her legs to the hollows behind her knees. Then he was touching and kissing her everywhere. The sated feeling of moments ago slipped away to be replaced by renewed desire as he laced his brushing caresses with random kisses, dropping them along her darkened skin wherever they happened to fall—on a breast, an inner elbow, a hip, her stomach . . .

She tensed, tightened her stomach muscles, and held a pent-up breath, sensing his destination. She reached for his shoulders to stop him, but it was too late. His tongue touched her intimately, leaving her feeling utterly vulnerable and undeniably prurient.

"Rick . . . I . . ." His hand reached blindly to cover her lips while his lambent touches sent currents of sensation firing her veins with new life. Resistance fled beneath the onslaught of sensations, and she fell back, a strangled sound issuing from her throat, until at last he knelt to her, entering the silken front of sensuality with easy grace. When he clutched her hips and pressed deep, a soft growl escaped his throat, then the dark was filled only with music and breathing and the magnificence they shared as his body blended into hers.

He murmured her name, interspersing it with endearments, and somehow the beats of their bodies matched, became rhythm and rhyme as she lay back, remembering the sheen of these muscles the first time she'd rubbed them with oil, picturing his perfect face as vividly as if the room were not cast into darkness.

Her fingers flexed into the flesh of his shoulders as he moved within her, taking her beyond the point of no return. And when her nails unconsciously dug in, he jerked her wrists down, pinning them against the cushions while together they thrust closer . . . closer . . . closer.

His breath was tortured, her voice a ragged plea as she begged, "Let . . . m . . . my . . . hands . . . g . . . go."

The pressure left her wrists, but her fingers remained clenched as she clung to his strong back while beat for beat she rode with him to their devastating climaxes.

Oh, it was good. Everything about it was good.

He, too, was trembling, trying to control it by pressing her hard against him, holding the back of her head with a widespread palm. They had slipped down, their bodies now wilting toward the floor. Finally they gave in to the inertia that dumped their sated limbs in a loose heap onto the shaggy rug.

The radio was still playing. It intruded now where before they'd been unconscious of it in the background. Side by side they rested, neither able to conjure up the strength to move, while tomorrow's weather was followed by a time check and a tuneful commercial for soft drinks. Then from the speakers came a guitar intro to a soulful melody and a man's voice singing into their intimate world: "When I'm stretched on the floor after loving once more with your skin pressing mine and we're tired and fine . . ."

The words broke into Allison's consciousness in an unwelcome reminder of the past. But this was Rick, not Jason! Yet he was lying just as the words of the song described, flat out on the floor, and the enormity of what they'd done together struck Allison. Committed. She'd committed herself to a man again by sharing the most intimate of acts. Almost as if it possessed a clairvoyance, the radio reminded her that once before she'd done this, trusted like this, only . . .

Rick's warm hand rested on the soft skin of her inner elbow, and slowly she eased away from his touch and left his side to search for her clothing in the dark.

"Allison?" She sensed how he'd braced up on an elbow, but she didn't answer, feeling along the seat of the sofa. Through the dark the song kept playing. Then a moment later she heard his heels thud across the floor toward the radio, and an angry hand slam against it, thrusting the room into silence. He found her again, but as his hand touched her shoulder, she ducked aside and evaded it.

"Allison, what's wrong?"

"Nothing."

"Don't lie to me." He touched her again, but she retreated to the sofa, curling up with her feet beneath her. The light switch sounded, and Allison flinched.

"Don't . . . don't turn the light on, please."

The light flooded over her shoulder from the table lamp behind her, revealing her strewn hair and withdrawn pose as Rick studied her.

"You want to talk about it?" he asked.

"Just . . . let it be." The only garment at hand was her jeans. She pulled them across her lap and slumped her shoulders as if to shield her naked breasts.

He leaned forward to touch her knee. "No, it's too important."

"Don't look at me." She huddled now, shivering while he hesitated uncertainly for a moment, then retrieved his shirt from the top of the stereo and draped it over her shivering arms and shoulders. He slipped into his pants, then returned to kneel on one knee before her, searching for words, for meanings, for reasons. But she remained closed against him as he tiredly rested an elbow on a knee and kneaded the bridge of his nose, waiting—for what, he didn't know. Insight perhaps, guidance, a hint of where to start.

"Allison, tell me about it. Tell me about him."

Her head snapped up. "It's none of your business. I told you, no questions. Just . . . leave me alone, Jas . . ." Realizing her slip, she cut the word in half.

"Is that his name . . . Jason?"

"I said don't probe, dammit! Don't try to ch—"

"Don't probe!" he shouted, coming to his feet, towering over her. "Don't probe?" He flung a palm angrily at the sofa cushions. "You just came close to calling me by his name and you say don't probe?" He laughed once, ruefully. "What the hell do you think I am, stupid? I heard your precious Five Senses song come on the radio, and I felt what it did to you. All of a sudden you weren't there any more. How do you expect me to react?"

"Please, I . . . I . . . we shouldn't have done this." She turned her eyes aside. "I think you should go."

She saw how he braced one hand on his waistband and locked his knees, his feet spread wide.

"I'll need my shirt," he stated coldly.

She waited, expecting him to yank it from her, dreading the moment when she'd be exposed to him again. Instead his angry footsteps moved across the hardwood floor to her bedroom. She heard the closet door open, then he came back, stood before her with her blue robe clenched in his hands, and repeated tightly, "I have to take my shirt." A hand reached out, and she thought she saw it tremble before she clamped her eyelids shut, and the cool air covered her naked skin.

He glanced at her arms, crossed now protectively over her breasts. "I want to fling this thing at you and tell you to go to hell, you know that?"

Her eyes opened and met his. He was so totally honest—why couldn't she be that honest about her feelings? He dropped the robe in her lap, then donned his shirt, tucked it in, and stood contemplatively. He sighed heavily at last, ran a hand through his hair, and squatted down beside the sofa again, studying the floor. "We can't drop it here, you know. We have to talk," he said.

"Not now, okay?" she asked tremulously.

He nodded. His knees cracked as he stood up again. "I'll call you."

Still he didn't go, but stood above her, looking down on her hair, which stood out like a dark nimbus in the light drenching her shoulder as she fought to hold back the tears.

"Hey," he asked huskily, "you gonna be all right?"

She nodded jerkily, once, and he turned away. She heard him pause at the door to pull on his boots, heard the snaps of his jacket, and knew he was watching her through the long silent pause before the door opened, then quietly closed behind him.

At its soft click Allison flung herself around and fell across the back of the sofa, burying her head in her arms. And there in her loneliness and confusion she cried. For Jason. For Rick. And for herself.

Chapter
NINE

RICK Lang had left his Hasselblad behind. Guilt stricken at how she'd treated him, Allison at first declined to use it. He didn't call on Monday or Tuesday, and by Wednesday the shots of the Winterfest came back from processing—crisp, clear and breathtaking. After viewing them, she found herself staring at the phone, wanting terribly to call him, to apologize. But she had hurt him so badly . . . so badly. She stared out the studio windows, seeing only Rick Lang, whom she'd likened to Jason when he was nothing at all like Jason. He cared so little about his looks, he hadn't even asked to see the transparencies of the book cover.

She sighed and turned back to her work—a layout for a Tiffany diamond. The engagement ring nestled within the petals of an apricot rose to which she had applied a single drop of water with an eyedropper. Against a backdrop of lush salmon satin, the composition was stunning. She glanced at the Hasselblad again, weakened, picked it up, and was loading it a moment later.

The diamond, the rose, and the camera again worked on Allison's conscience, and she promised herself she'd call Rick and apologize as soon as she got home. But before she finished the series of photos the phone rang, and Mattie said, "Prepare yourself, kiddo, I've got some news you aren't going to like."

"What?"

"Remember that series of shots you took of Jason last fall—the ones in the Harris tweeds?"

"Of course I remember."

"Well, get ready for a surprise—they're in this month's *Gentlemen's Review*."

The shock set Allison in her chair with a plop. "What!"

"You heard me right. They're in this month's *GR*."

"B . . . but that's impossible! He only stole them a few weeks ago."

"Apparently not. It appears he lifted them months ago and submitted them then. When did you realize they were missing?"

A sick feeling made Allison's stomach go hollow. "When he left, of course. I wasn't running to the files daily while he was living with me to see if his intentions were honorable or not."

"Well, the creep was about as honorable as Judas Iscariot! The photo credit lists the photographer as Herbert Wells."

"Undoubtedly with a post office box in some eastern city to which *GR* was instructed to send the handsome paycheck," Allison surmised bitterly.

"You're going to tell the police, aren't you?"

Allison sighed uselessly. "Without the negatives to prove the originals were mine?"

There was silence, then Mattie's sympathetic voice. "Listen, honey, I'm really sorry I had to give you the bad news."

"Yeah, sure," said the lifeless voice in the wide, drafty, echoey studio.

Allison hung up and shot to her feet, taking a defiant, angry stance as she stared unseeingly at the glittering diamond that seemed to wink hauntingly from the velvety folds of the rose. Two diamond-hard tears glittered from Allison's eyes.

Damn you, Jason, you bastard! Even while you were taking me to bed night after night you were lying all the time, using your body to get me to do exactly what you **wanted. Well, you certainly saw me coming! You** must've been standing on the sidewalk watching while this stupid little South Dakota farm girl came rolling off the turnip truck!

I fell for your line like some sex-starved ninny, while you stole the one thing that meant more to me than even you. All those transparencies—my God!—all of them good enough for publication, while I never suspected. But you knew, didn't you? You knew and you used me. You picked my body and my files clean and made sure I'd know exactly how, by selling them to *GR!*

Where are you now? Laughing in some other woman's arms while you tell her about the ignorant little farm wench from Watertown?

It all flooded back, redoubling Allison's sick realization of how gullible she'd been—of all the times she'd fawned over his body, adored it, both in clothing before the lens and out of it in bed. What a fool she'd been not to see how one-sided her affection was. He took her every compliment as if it were his due while giving back nothing but his body. And that he gave with a hint of smugness, as if doing her a favor.

She cringed now at the memory of how openly she'd displayed her need, her desire, her love. For she *had* loved him. That's what hurt the most. She had. And Jason had fed off her, figuratively as well as literally, for she'd paid all the bills as long as he posed, posed, posed, while she collected the portfolio of photos he was systematically rifling all along.

She lived again the anguish and disbelief of that afternoon she'd returned to the apartment to find his message scrawled across the bottom of the picture on the easel. How typical of him to leave his parting message in that way, as if she were some adolescent groupie.

Allison sighed, deep and long, then dropped to her desk chair forlornly. Jason Ederlie had done it all to her, everything a man could possibly do to a woman. He'd taken all a man could take, left as little as a man could leave.

Well, she'd learned her lesson but good. She'd been taken in once by a stunning face and a talented body, but no man would ever reduce her this way again. Not even Rick Lang! Whether he doled out kisses like Eros himself, nobody was going to worm his way into her heart or her bed or her files again!

The telephone rang once more that afternoon. When Allison recognized Rick's voice, she told him this was the answering service and that she would have Ms. Scott return his call. There followed a puzzled hesitation before he thanked her and hung up.

At home that night during supper Allison's phone rang twice. Later she lay in bed listening to its jangling insistence for the fourth time since she'd gotten

LaVYRLE SPENCER

home. Determinedly she buried her head under the pillow.

The following morning her answering service reported that a man named Rick Lang had been calling and was becoming abusive to the woman on duty, who could not make him believe they weren't withholding his messages from Ms. Scott.

Late Thursday Allison made the sudden decision to go to Watertown for the weekend. But she was restless and irritable even there, for the farmhouse felt confining. She wished she could talk to her mother about Jason and Rick, but her mother would never understand Allison's having had a sexual relationship with a man before marriage, much less having lived with him for the better part of a year. Sexual intercourse had never, never been a discussed subject at home, and Allison knew her mother would be extremely uncomfortable to confront it with her daughter, even now.

Allison's married brother Wendell farmed nearby, but they weren't close enough for her to seek his counsel either. Then, too, every time Allison's mother looked at her it was with a shake of the head as she declared, "Land, you're nothing but skin and bones, girl." At mealtime the woman invariably added another spoonful from each dish after Allison had already filled her plate.

Finally over Sunday breakfast Allison's irritation

churned out of control, and she exploded, "Dammit, Mother, I'm twenty-five years old! I don't need any help deciding how many scrambled eggs to eat for breakfast!"

The stunned silence that followed left Allison feeling guilty and far less adult than she claimed to be. She returned to the city more discontent than ever, and bearing one more niggling burden of guilt.

She was sitting in her empty, silent apartment eating a TV dinner that tasted like plastic when the phone rang. She glared at it, dumped her unfinished food into the garbage can, and went to do her washing. The damn phone rang with extreme regularity through three loads of washing and the ironing, too. She was sure it was Rick, but refused to take the phone off the hook, and let him know she was home.

But the ringing finally raised her hackles beyond soothing. She yanked the receiver up and blared, "Yes, yes, yes! What do you want!"

There was a moment of silence, then his voice. "Allison?"

"Yes?"

"Just where in the hell have you been for three days!" he exploded.

"I went home to South Dakota."

"While you let me wonder if you'd dropped off the face of the earth!"

"I didn't want to see you or talk to you," she explained expressionlessly.

"Oh, well, that's just dandy! You didn't want to see me! Just like that! Did you happen to think I might be going crazy worrying about you while you traipsed off and ignored my calls!"

He was so angry the receiver seemed to quiver in her palm. Allison's hand was shaking too as she backed up against the wall, let her eyes droop shut, sighed, and slid down until her butt hit the floor. "No," she answered wearily, "no, I didn't stop to consider that. I'm sorry."

"Well, you should be, for crissakes," he raged on. "You don't just disappear into thin air to leave a man wondering if you're alive or dead or what the hell is going through your impossible female head. You were pretty damned upset when I left you the other night, you know. Did you think I—"

"I said I was sorry!" she hissed.

"Well, dammit, I was worried sick! I've been up to your apartment no less than eight times in the last three days, and all the people downstairs could tell me was that they hadn't seen you since sometime Thursday morning, and they didn't know where you'd gone. And I couldn't get one damn thing out of your answering service except some catty little snoot placating me with 'I'm sorry, Mr. Lang, but we've given her all your messages.' So just what the hell kind of game are you playing!"

"It's no game," Allison assured him. "We had some laughs together and took a few pictures and ended up making love, that's all. That doesn't constitute a commitment of any kind. It was just a . . . a mistake."

"Just a mistake," Rick repeated, thunderstruck, his voice now holding a sharp edge of hurt. "You call what happened between us a mistake? Who the hell are you trying to kid, Allison?"

"It *was* a mistake for me. It's too . . ." She stopped, drew a deep breath, and went on. "I can't see you anymore, Rick. I'm sorry, I'm just not as resilient as I thought I was. I can't forget that fast—"

"Forget what! Something I did or something *he* did? I'm not him, damn it, yet you're judging me as if I were! If you're going to judge a man, at least do it on his own merits and shortcomings instead of someone else's."

Damn him, he was right! But the full sting of Jason's duplicity was too fresh within Allison to allow her to feel unthreatened by the thought of committing herself to a new relationship. To commit was to become vulnerable again.

"So why are you wasting your time on me?" It hurt, it hurt, having to say those words to him. And even across the telephone wire she could tell they hurt him, too.

"I don't know. I felt what we did together *does* constitute a commitment, and I thought you were the kind of woman who felt the same way, but apparently I was wrong." A pause followed, then he muttered, "Oh, hell," and his voice grew persuasive. "I don't know how to say this, but you and I spent some hours together that were far, far above the ordinary for first times. We worked and laughed and learned we had a lot in common. And after such a great day last Sunday, the way we ended it was as natural an ending as . . . as . . . you know what I'm talking about, Allison. We're good together, so I kissed you and you kissed me back and we made love . . ." His voice had gone low and gruff. "And don't lie to me. It was like fireworks." She heard him swallow. "And then you ran, and I deserve some answers, Allison. I have a right to know why."

"Because I'm afraid, okay?" she answered truthfully.

"Tell me what Jason—"

"I don't understand why you're bothering. I'm not even a very good . . ." But abruptly she gulped to a halt.

"Lover?" he filled in. "Is that what you were going to say? Because if it is, you might be interested in knowing that not every guy thinks of that first. Some people honestly look for the person inside the body first. Some people actually base their feelings on more than just superficial appearances." He paused. "And you are a hell of a good lover."

"Stop it! Stop it! You want to know why I'm afraid to trust you, I'll tell you why. Because I trusted Jason

Ederlie and all I got for it was taken. We lived together and I paid his way. Like a stupid, lovesick fool I took him in and stroked his ego and let him live scot-free off me, thinking all the time we were working toward . . . toward something permanent. He posed for me. Oh, did he pose! And he knew his charms very well. I laid my whole future on the line with him, and one day I walked into this house and found him gone—lock, stock, and negatives! You want to know why I'm afraid to commit myself to a man again? Open up this month's issue of *Gentlemen's Review* and find out. You'll recognize his face—it's the one from my files. They say a picture is worth a thousand words—well, in *GR* it's also worth about a thousand dollars and a fixed career, and there's a whole layout of them. Only the photo credit, you'll note, is not quite accurate!"

By now Allison was quivering, viewing the chrome legs of the dining room chairs through a blur of angry tears.

"All that doesn't change one thing that's gone on between you and me, Allison, because it's past. It's done. What about what we shared?"

"What about it?" she retorted, wanting to draw back the words, but unable to, hurting him, hurting herself.

First came stunned, hurt silence, then carefully controlled words. "Nothing—nothing at all. I've been talk-

ing to the wrong girl all night long. And I mean *girl!*
Why don't you grow up, Allison, and stop blaming the
rest of the world for one man's transgressions? Then
maybe you'll find somebody *worthy* of your lofty attention!"

Without saying good-bye, Rick Lang hung up.

THE days and weeks that followed were filled with the
deepest despair Allison had ever known, deeper than
that she'd suffered when Jason deserted her, for then
she'd been fortified by justifiable anger. Now she had no
blame to lay on Rick Lang and thereby assuage her own
shortcomings.

Rick had done nothing to earn her callous rejection—
nothing. Her own insecurity had caused her to treat him
so cruelly. A hundred times a day she considered calling
him, apologizing, telling him it wasn't his fault, that he
was innocent of everything she had accused him of. But
she was utterly ashamed of how she'd acted. And now,
too, she felt unworthy of him.

The vision of Rick filled her thoughts as the days
stretched into weeks. In her memories she no longer
searched for flaws, for he possessed none, none with
which he had ever sought to hurt her, to dominate her,
even to bolster his own ego. Those were crutches Jason
had used—Jason, not Rick. He had entered the relationship honestly; it was she who had hidden truths from

him and disguised her fears behind a façade of wariness and distrust.

Ah, what a sorry human being she was. She deserved the hurt and the sense of loss she now suffered as the dreary days of February paraded past and she heard nothing from Rick Lang.

The photographs of their day at the Winterfest brought painful memories of what she had so carelessly cast aside. Leafing through them one day, she recalled a time she now longed for, a man she now longed for, who had treated her decently, honorably. In a spate of self-disgust she threw the pictures across her desk and lowered her head to her arms to cry again.

She was so tired of crying.

When she blew her nose and dried her eyes, she felt better. Resting her chin on a fist on the desktop, she scanned again the scattered scenes with their bright colors and bittersweet memories.

Call him, call him, a lonely voice cried.

He'll have nothing to say—you've hurt him too badly.

Apologize, came the taunting, haunting voice.

After the way you treated him? You have no right to call him.

Her head came up off her fist, and she collected the photos, sniffling still, and rubbed a wrist under her eyes and laid the collection in a row. Studying them in a series, she realized they were remarkably well-done, giving an overall effect of vibrant Minnesotans hard at play in the midst of an icy winter's day.

On a sudden impulse she dashed off a cover letter and jammed them into an envelope along with it, and put them in the mail to *Mpls./St. Paul* magazine.

To Allison's amazement, she received a call three days later from a man who wanted to buy the series for their April issue.

But the joy she would otherwise have basked in was dulled by the fact that she couldn't share it with Rick, who had been so much a part of that day. When Allison hung up the phone, she stood for long minutes, hands hugging her thin hips through tight jeans pockets as she stared at the phone.

Again she had the sudden urge to call him and tell him the news. But once more she felt guilty and undeserving and decided against it.

The Hasselblad was still here. She worked with it daily, realizing she must return it, afraid to call and tell him he could either come and get it or she would take it to his place.

On the first day of March she returned home to find an envelope with strange handwriting in her mailbox. Racing up the stairs, she flung off her cap and scarf, her heart warming, warning—it's from him! It's from him!

She curled her feet beneath her on the sofa, studying the writing. The envelope was pink. She began to rip it open, then suddenly changed her mind, wanting to keep it flawless and neat if it truly were from him. She found a knife in the kitchen and slit the envelope open carefully.

Back on the sofa she slipped the greeting card slowly from its holder. There came into view a hand-painted card done in pastel watercolors of a single stalk of forget-me-nots forcing their way up between an old brick wall and a weathered gnarl of driftwood around which wild grasses waved in dappled shadow.

Even before she opened it, Allison's eyes had filled with tears. She ran her fingertips over the rough texture of the watercolor paper, realizing it was the first of his work she'd seen.

A wildlife artist, he'd said, but she'd never asked once to see his work, never displayed an interest in it at all. Yet she'd heartlessly accused *him* of egoism! She was the egotist, so wrapped up in her own career she'd never bothered to ask about his.

Considering the sensitivity that radiated from the simple drawing, she realized an enormous truth—Rick Lang didn't give a damn about his physical appearance and did not feed off it, because it was wholly secondary to what was most important in his life—his art.

She opened the folded sheet. His writing, done with black ink and calligraphy pen, slanted across the page: *I haven't forgotten. Rick.*

Allison clamped a hand over her mouth, swallowing repeatedly at the sudden surge of emotion that welled up in her throat. His face came back, beguiling, entreating.

No, Rick, I haven't forgotten either, but I'm so ashamed, how can I face you again?

She sat there for a long time with her legs drawn up tightly against her chest, thinking of him, remembering, reliving all the enjoyable hours spent with him, their teasing and laughter, the disastrous omelette, their exuberant forays into the winter days, the night they'd shared that wonderful sense of oneness after the studio session, and, of course, the night he'd made love to her.

His words came back clearly. "I'm still one of those guys who wants to do the pursuing." She now wanted so badly to call him, but the memory of those words stopped her.

She glanced at the telephone and decided that if he wanted to see her again, he'd call.

I N mid-March she sent him a brief note telling him she'd leave the Hasselblad at the North Star Modeling Agency, and he could pick it up there. She debated for a long time before adding, "I loved your card. You're gifted with a paintbrush." Debating again about how to sign it, she finally decided on, "Yours, A."

* * *

THE last two weeks of March dragged past. The buds on the trees along Nicollet Mall were bursting with new life, ready to sprout greenery into the heart of downtown Minneapolis, which was vibrant with expectancy now that spring was just around the corner. In downtown bank plazas noontime fashion shows offered spring garments in an array of bright colors—short sleeved and breezy in anticipation of the balmy season ahead.

Allison bought a chic suit of pale yellow linen to take home to Watertown for Easter, which fell in mid-April. But the new suit did little to lift her spirits as day after day she hoped to find another letter in her mailbox from Rick. But none came.

She broke down in early April and tried calling him for three days in a row, but got no answer.

Carefully nonchalant, she went to North Star's office one day to ask Mattie if Rick Lang had come by to pick up his camera.

"Sure did," Mattie answered. "Said he was happy to have it back because he was going home, wherever that is, to get some spring shots for his files."

Depressed at the idea of his being miles away, in a town where she'd never been, Allison submerged herself in work, trying to put him out of her mind.

Hathaway Books called, saying they loved the cover

concept and photography she'd done and offering her a
contract to do two more. It should have elated Allison,
but while she was happy, that ebullient feeling she'd expected to experience at a time like this was curiously
absent.

IN mid-April another envelope bearing Rick's writing
showed up in the mail—a hastily scrawled pencil
sketch of a fawn standing beneath a leafless tree. Inside
he'd written, "I've been out of town, reevaluating. Just
got back and saw the spread in *Mpls./St. Paul.* Congratulations! You, too, are gifted . . . with my Hasselblad.
Yours, Rick."

The spirits that had lain unlifted by either the new
spring suit or the two-book contract offer were buoyed
to the heights by his simple message.

Again she considered calling him, but studied the
word "reevaluating" and decided it was best to leave
the pursuing to him, if he ever decided to see her
again.

Easter came and at the last minute before leaving
town on Good Friday, Allison picked up an Easter card
at the drugstore and addressed it to him, writing beneath
the printed message, "I, too, am reevaluating. Yours, Allison."

Spending two days at home this time, Allison remembered Rick's analysis of her parents' motives and found herself less critical of them, enjoying her weekend immensely.

The winter wheat was already sprouting in the limitless fields around the farmhouse, and she took time for a long walk through them, evaluating not only herself but also Rick, their relationship, and the far too great importance she had put on the treatment given her by Jason Ederlie.

What was she afraid of?

The answer, she found now, was nothing! She wasn't afraid; she was eager. She wanted the chance to see Rick Lang again, to apologize, to laugh with him, make love with him if he would have her, and to prove that she was willing to judge him for himself alone, not by measuring him against a man who, during the past few months, had become only a vague recollection and whose memory had almost ceased to bring the hurt and despondency it once had.

No word came again until the first of May. A long, narrow, hand-painted card bearing a basket of mayflowers with a ribbon tied to its handle, streamers flying breezily in the wind.

Inside it said, "There's an old May Day tradition that if a girl likes a boy, she leaves a May basket on his step, rings his doorbell, then runs, in the hopes that he'll catch her and kiss her. I'm not sure if boys are allowed to do the same thing, but . . . Love, Rick."

Allison's cheeks grew as pink as the May blossoms on his painting, and a glorious smile lit her face. She felt as if a bouquet of flowers had burst to profusion within her very heart. Breathing became suddenly difficult, and she turned, studying the sofa in her bright living room where late afternoon sun now streamed through the windows of the sun porch, whose French doors were opened.

She remembered Rick here in his many poses and knew beyond a doubt that he would be here again . . . soon.

She would invite him over for supper, she thought, immediately tossing the idea out as too forward. Not here, not in this place where memories of the past might come to threaten. They needed neutral territory on which to meet and assess the changes they were sure to find in each other.

Unsure of what his message meant, she was still reluctant to be the one to call him. Rick Lang, pursuer, she thought with a smile.

She waited another day, and in the mail at the studio there arrived the answer to her quandary—the announcement of a two-day symposium and workshop at University of Wisconsin-Madison, at which the keynote speaker would be Roberto Finelli, a renowned

instructor of photography from Brooks Institute in
Santa Barbara.

Subject: Photographing People for Profit
Requirements: 35mm camera, colored film, and a
model of your choice
Dates: May 19–20
Registration Fee: $160.00
Meals: Available at the college cafeteria at student
rates
Lodging: Not arranged for, hotels and motels
available in vicinity near the campus

Odd how insignificant her lifetime dream of meeting
Finelli suddenly seemed when offered beside the opportunity of seeing Rick Lang again, of working with him
and in the process rectifying the mistake she'd made
with him.

The hands of the clock seemed to creep by so slowly
that at one point Allison actually called for correct
time, verifying that it was her own eagerness and not
some electrical malfunction that made the hours move
so slowly. She could have called Rick from the studio,
but for some reason she wanted to be at home when
she did.

But when five o'clock finally arrived and Allison got
home, she dawdled unnecessarily through a tuna salad
sandwich, reaching for the phone three times while the

heartbeats in her throat threatened to choke her. Each time she pulled back the sweating hand, wiping it on her thigh, turning around to pace the living room and work up her courage.

He wouldn't be home, she thought frantically. Or he might be home but have somebody else with him and not be able to talk. Or maybe he would be able to talk but would refuse—then what?

Chicken, Allison?

Damn right, I'm chicken!

Then don't call—spend the rest of your life wishing you had!

Oh shut up, I'll do it when I'm good and ready!

Ha!

He would have called if he wanted to see me.

You're the one who threw him out, remember!

But he said he's old-fashioned about these things.

He's made it abundantly clear he wants to see you.

She grabbed the phone and dialed so fast she had no chance to change her mind. Waiting while it rang, she wildly wished he wouldn't be home, for she had no idea how to begin.

"Hello?"

She clutched the phone, but not a word squeaked through her throat.

"Hello? . . . Hello?"

"Rick?" Was that her voice, so cool, so low, so controlled, when her heart was thumping out of her chest?

A long pause, then his surprised voice. "Allison?"

"Yeah . . . hi."

"Hi yourself." The ensuing silence seemed to stretch across light-years of time before he added, "I pretty much gave up hope of hearing from you again."

"I gave up hope of hearing from you."

Silence roared along, carrying her thumping heart with it. He began to say something but had a frog in his throat and had to clear it to start again. "So how are you doing?"

"Better."

"Obviously, with the sale to *Mpls./St. Paul* and everything. The pictures were really great, I mean that. I couldn't believe it when I opened my copy and saw them."

"It . . . it was a surprise when they called to say they'd buy them. I . . . well, I sent them off on kind of an impulse, you know?"

"Lucky impulse."

"Yeah . . . yeah, lucky."

She shrugged as if he could see her and stared at the floor between her feet, but neither of them seemed able to think of anything more to say now that that subject was exhausted.

"Oh, guess what!" she said, remembering. "Hathaway offered me a contract to do two more book covers!"

"Hey, congratulations! Now you'll know where next month's groceries are coming from, and the month's after that."

Old simple words from their past—did he forget nothing?—but the memories they conjured up were rife with other things she wanted them to say to one another.

Finally Allison remembered what she'd called for.

"Listen, are you still modeling?"

"Sure. It pays the bills, same as always."

"Would you like a job?"

"Sure."

"For me?"

To Rick she sounded uncertain, as if she thought he might say no when he found out who it was for. "Why not?" he asked.

"It's not the regular kind of job, you know—I mean, not the book covers again, but I figure we can both learn a little something if we do it together. I mean, it's a workshop and symposium down at University of Wisconsin called Photographing People for Profit. The guest speaker is going to be Roberto Finelli. I've . . . well, I've always wanted a chance to meet him." Her words tumbled out one after the other to hide her nervousness.

"When is it?"

"May nineteenth and twentieth."

"Two full days?"

She realized the implications of staying overnight and swallowed hard, wondering what he was thinking.

"Yeah," she finally answered, trying to sound non-committal. He's going to say no! He's going to say no! she thought, her palms now sweating profusely, her cheeks already flushing with embarrassment.

"It sounds fun."

The sun burst forth inside her head with a blazing flash of wonder.

"It does?" Her lips dropped open, her eyes were wide with pleasant shock.

"Of course it does. Did you think I'd refuse?" She thought she detected a slight lilt of teasing in his question.

"I . . . I wasn't sure." She had clapped one hand over the top of her head to hold it on. You like to do the pursuing, she thought—you told me so!

"You'll have to tell me what kind of clothes to wear," he was saying, while she controlled her euphoria in order to settle the final details.

They made plans for her to pick him up at four A.M. on the appointed day. This settled, there came a lull in the conversation.

Allison was on her feet, pacing the length of the phone cord. She stopped and stared at the daybed on the sun porch, wondering if summer would find them on it. "Well . . ." she muttered stupidly.

Well, she thought . . . *well?* Is that all you can think of to say, *well!* Think of some bright, witty ending to this conversation, Scott!

He cleared his throat and said, "Yeah . . . well."

Silence.

Allison's palms were sweating. She wiped them on her thighs. "I'll see you on the nineteenth then."

"The nineteenth," he repeated. "Good-bye."

"Good-bye."

But Allison didn't want to be the first one to hang up. She stood in the sunset-washed living room, staring at the spot where they'd made love, hugging the receiver to her ear, listening to him breathe. After a long, long moment she lowered the receiver and pressed it firmly between her breasts, her heart racing, a feeling of imminent fullness overpowering her senses.

"Rick Lang, I love you," she whispered to the picture of him behind her closed eyelids, unsure if he could hear the muffled words or the crazy commotion of her heart, suddenly not caring if he knew the full extent of her feelings for him.

She lifted the receiver to her ear again and listened, but could not be sure if he was still there. At last she hung up.

Chapter
TEN

THE morning of May nineteenth had not yet dawned when Allison Scott drove her Chevy van through the winding streets of the elegant old part of Minneapolis called Kenwood. Situated in the hills behind the Walker Art Center and the Guthrie Theater, it was once home to the city's oldest monied families. But in more recent years the founding families had moved to lake-shore estates, and Kenwood had been captured by young architects, lawyers, and doctors who'd brought new life, and children, to the staid, old sector.

Thick wooded hills and winding streets twisted through the area, making addresses hard to find. But Allison followed Rick's precise instructions through the sleeping hulks of old homes that in the daytime drew sightseers to admire cupolas, porches, banisters, turrets, carriage houses, dormers, gables, and more, for no two homes in the area were alike.

Just off Kenwood Parkway Allison found the designated street and number, an elegant old three-story building of English Tudor styling buried beneath overhanging elms, its front door flanked by soldier-straight bushes trimmed to military precision. A sidewalk wound its way around to the back of the house, and Allison followed it beside a high wall of honeysuckle hedge that dripped dew, its full blossoms giving off a heady scent.

A light was on above a second-story door much like hers, and she took the steps with a queer sense of familiarity, of coming home. He'd never told her he lived in a place so much like her own.

She paused, searching for a bell. There was none, but she clutched the tiny woven Easter basket in her hands, wondering if it was wise to give it to him after all. It was large enough to hold only one Easter egg, which it had when her brother Wendell's little daughter had given it to her Aunt Allison with beaming pride, declaring she had dyed the egg herself.

The basket now held two candy kisses and a tiny cluster of lilies of the valley that Allison had stolen from her landlady's garden and tied with a small pink grosgrain ribbon.

Allison drew a deep, deep breath, held it for an interminable length of time, let it gush out, then soundly rapped on the door.

She heard footsteps approaching on the opposite side, and her heart threatened to stop up her throat.

The door opened, and she forgot the basket, forgot the words she'd rehearsed, forgot the businesslike air she'd vowed to maintain, forgot everything except Rick Lang, standing before her in a pair of crisply ironed blue jeans with an open-necked white shirt underneath a flawless lightweight sport coat of muted spring plaid that gaped away from his ribs as his hand hung on the edge of the door.

Through Allison's tumult of emotions it struck her that he'd dressed up for her. His hair, she thought—he had combed his hair! How could she ever have imagined it would be folly to touch a comb to it? She'd never seen such a tempting head of hair in her life. It was blow-combed to a neat feathered perfection, covering the tips of his ears on its backward sweep, touching his forehead as it fell faultlessly forward.

Rick Lang neither smiled nor stepped back nor spoke, but studied her with an expression that told Allison little about what he was thinking.

At last she came to her senses. "Good morning." Her voice sounded pinched and squeaky.

"Good morning." His sounded deep and even.

Again Allison struggled to find something to say. Suddenly she jumped as if she'd just touched an electric fence and thrust the silly little basket forward.

"Here . . . for you." She added a quavering smile. "But I'm not running."

He looked down, smiled, and slowly reached out for the basket, hooking its tiny handle over a single index finger.

Immediately she clasped both hands behind her back.

He looked up with a grin. "Of course not. It's not May Day."

She felt herself blushing and cast about for a quick reply, but none came. Still clutching her hands behind her, Allison leaned forward from the waist, peering around him inquisitively. "Mmm . . . nice house. It reminds me of mine."

He stepped back quickly. "Mine doesn't have a sun porch, and somebody covered up all the hardwood floors with these ugly brown carpets, but it's roomy, close to town, and has all the conveniences."

"Yes, it's nice." *Nice*, she thought . . . you *ninny!* "It's really . . ." Allison stopped her examination of the premises. Realizing it had grown silent behind her, she turned to find his eyes following her with a hint of amusement in their expression.

"You were about to say?" he prompted.

"I . . . nothing." She ordered the blood to stop rushing to her head.

"We'd better get going if we're going to make it to Madison by ten." He turned away and headed toward a door leading off the opposite side of the living room. "Be right back," he called over his shoulder.

She scanned the room again, wishing she had hours to study it so that she might learn of him, his likes, his ways. An easel stood near a north window, but it was turned to catch the window's light, and she couldn't see what he was working on. There were deep leather chairs and a matching davenport and bookcases with hundreds of items other than books. His old, worn letter jacket lay across the back of one of the chairs. She walked over and touched it lightly.

"Ready?" he asked.

She jerked her hand back as if he'd caught her stealing. "Yes."

He held a suitcase in one hand, a zippered clothing bag slung over the opposite shoulder, and in the button-hole of his jacket lapel he'd stuck the cluster of lilies of the valley.

She pulled her eyes away from the flowers with an effort and came forward. "Here, I can take something."

She reached for the garment bag, but he said, "No, I'll get that, but you can take this." There was some confusion while he attempted to shrug a wide woven strap from his shoulder, but it got tangled in the ends of the hangers.

LaVYRLE SPENCER

At last it was free and in her hands. "The Hassel-blad?" she asked, looking up with surprise in her face.

"What else?" He smiled.

"But—"

"When she's working under Finelli for the first time, a woman ought to be really turned on, right?"

She beamed radiantly, hung the wide strap over her shoulder, and hugged the case protectively against her belly. "Thanks, Rick, I'll treat it like spun glass."

He stepped out onto the landing, set his suitcase down, and held the door, waiting for her to pass before him. "If I remember right," Rick teased, "that's where all this started."

As she crossed in front of him, she caught the intoxicating drift of lily of the valley, and it did little to still the heart that beat at double time, because she was with him again.

They stowed his gear in the back of the van. Rick slammed the doors shut and asked, "You want me to drive?"

"I'd love it."

She dropped the keys into his palm, and a minute later they were backing down the driveway, heading through the sleeping city toward the interstate.

"I've got coffee." She twisted around in her seat and dug out a thermos and chubby earthen mugs while he glanced sideways briefly, then back to the road,

226

checking the rearview mirror as the scent of coffee filled the van.

"One black . . . one with sugar," he remembered, reminding Allison of the first time they'd shared coffee this way. But his eyes remained on the road as he reached blindly and she placed the mug in his hand.

The horrible uncertainty of her first moments with him were gone, spinning farther into the distance as the miles rolled away beneath the wheels. She slumped back in her bucket seat, resting one high-heeled boot against the corner of the dash, balancing the coffee mug on her stomach. Occasionally she sipped, but mostly she basked in a feeling of supreme well-being at going off with him alone, attuned to his nearness, covertly watching his familiar hand on the wheel, listening to him sip his coffee now and then.

Rick, meanwhile, glanced time and again at the blue denim stretched tightly over her upraised knee and occasionally at the coffee mug resting on her stomach. At first only the lights from the dashboard illuminated the outline of her legs, but within half an hour the first strands of dawn lit the eastern sky as they headed directly into the sunrise. It was one of those explosive dawns that splash across the sky in layers of blue, pink, and orange. As the sun slipped above the horizon, they crossed the border into Wisconsin.

Rick turned to find Allison's cup slipping sideways.

He smiled to himself, turning lazy eyes toward her sleeping face. He had time for a longer, more intimate look as she slept trustfully beside him. He scanned her body with its chin settled onto a shoulder, that shoulder wedged at an uncomfortable angle in the corner of the seat, while her upraised knee swung indolently back and forth with the motion of the vehicle. The way she was scrunched up made her blouse buckle away from her chest. A shadowed hollow invited his eyes, and inside he saw a wisp of white lace. His eyes moved back to the road momentarily.

Her cup slipped farther askance and he reached to slide it from her fingers, but as it slipped away she jerked awake and sat up, looking sheepish.

"It's okay, go back to sleep."

"No, I'm not tired. I slept like a log last night."

He grinned and turned back to the road, making no comment while she wondered how he could possibly believe such a fat lie!

She sat up, entwined her fingers, and stretched her palms toward her knees, writhing a little, stiff-elbowed, and catlike.

"Looks like we're in for a knockout sunrise," Rick observed.

"Mmm . . . and I nearly missed it." She scanned the eastern horizon from north to south, her artist's eye appreciating this masterpiece the more for sharing it with him. She leaned forward, clasping her hands back to back between her knees, and savored being with him.

Wisconsin was devastatingly beautiful in its May costume. Fields of freshly tilled soil rolled along like flags waving in the wind, interspersed with blankets of budding forests where an occasional burst of wild plum blossoms could be seen in the distance. Immense promontories of sharp, gray rock loomed above the roadside, high and straight, their tops flat. They were awesome.

"It seems as if there should be an Indian on top of every one of them," Allison observed, "sitting there on a painted pony with a feathered lance in his hand."

"I've often thought the same thing myself."

Still they spoke of nothing personal. The remainder of the trip passed in companionable silence, but Allison knew they were only delaying what could inevitably not be delayed.

As they turned off the interstate at the Madison exit and followed Washington Avenue straight into the heart of the city, the dome of the state Capitol proudly guided them to its very center, seemingly built in the middle of the highway. They circled the Capitol grounds on quaint city streets arranged like a spiderweb around it.

The college town was bustling, its sidewalks swarming with students on bikes and on foot, bare armed, hurrying through the warm spring weather.

Allison and Rick found the correct building, parked the van and collected the Hasselblad, its equipment bag, and Allison's clipboard.

Finelli in the flesh inspired every photographer there with his opening speech and the narrative that accompanied a slide presentation of some of his most stunning work, many famous faces from film stars to politicians, cover girls to cardinals.

The lunch break came all too soon. Rick and Allison shared it in the campus cafeteria. Allison had difficulty coming down from the high inspired by the man who epitomized success in her chosen field.

Rick's voice repeated her name for the second time. "Allison?"

"Hmm?" She came up from her fanciful world where success was wholly achievable, pulling her eyes from her bowl of chili and grilled cheese sandwich to find Rick laughing at her.

"Hey there, dreamy, you haven't got Finelli's job yet. We have a workshop to attend and pictures to take. You gonna sit there and dream in your chili all day?"

She braced her chin on a palm and smiled dimly. "I will one day—have his job, I mean. Just you watch and see."

DURING the actual workshop cameras were set up in various lighting situations and personalized guid-

ance given to the photographers, allowing them to experiment with newly marketed equipment and various
techniques. Ideas were exchanged freely, live models
wandered about, and the country's most noted teachers
of photography gave advice and inspiration.

Allison looked up to see Rick approaching after having changed his clothes. He came striding toward her in
a set of clothes the likes of which she'd never seen on
him before. She was stunned. He was dressed in a thick-
textured sweater of pale gray with a bulky collar; dress
trousers of smooth navy gabardine, slightly pleated at
the waist; a small-collared button-down dress shirt of
pale smoky blue; highly polished black loafers; a gold
identification bracelet with a large-linked chain; and a
pendant bearing his sign of the zodiac—Aries—lying
just below the hollow of his throat, nestled in the pale
gold hair above his open collar.

"I'm ready," he announced quietly.

Wow, so am I! she thought, then realized her mouth
was hanging open and shut it with a snap. He moved
to the camera case to take out extra backs for the Hasselblad, while her eyes followed him like those of a
hungry puppy. As he stepped close to show her how to
load the several backs in advance, the scent of his aftershave set her quivering. "Each roll has only twelve
shots, you know, so I thought I'd bring the extra
backs. You can preload them," he said. But it was hard
for her to concentrate on the words. She watched his

long fingers showing her how to line up two double dots on the back of the camera if she wanted to double expose.

With an effort Allison forced her mind from Rick Lang to the business at hand. The renowned Finelli offered advice on back-lighting the hair with a colored filter to achieve a sunset effect. She produced the color print of the book cover, showing how she'd used the same technique with blue filters to create the effect of moon glow. He complimented her, watched as she proceeded, and offered kindly, "Young lady, it looks to me like you're wasting your time here. I'll move along to someone who needs my advice."

She looked up to see Rick stepping toward her. "Mind if I see that?"

She handed it to him silently, and they both studied Rick Lang leaning over Vivien Zuchinski with his hand near the side of her breast.

"It's damn good," he said quickly.

She looked at his temple as he studied the picture. "You're damn good." Before he could look into her eyes, she turned back to the camera.

By the end of the day's workshops it was four P.M. and both Allison and Rick were exhausted, yet curiously exhilarated. Heading back toward the van, he asked, "Is this going to be one of those nights when you're too high to sleep?"

She squeezed her eyes shut, opened them again, flung her arms wide, and bubbled joyously, "Yes! Yes! Yes!"

He watched the back of her hair swinging as she walked a step ahead of him, so energized she seemed ready to do cartwheels up the sidewalk.

"In that case I won't be keeping you from sleeping if I take you out to dinner."

"Oh, you don't have to do that." She turned to insist, but found her shoulder nearly colliding with his chest as he walked along, the sweater slung over his shoulder on two fingers.

"I know. I want to."

They studied each other for a silent moment. "Yeah?" she inquired cutely.

"Yeah," he repeated, grinning at her tilted chin and giving her a slow-motion mock punch on the jaw.

"Don't mind if I do," she decided. "I hardly touched my lunch, I was so off in another world. Sorry I get that way, but I can't help it. Lord, but I'm half starved, and I just realized it when you mentioned dinner."

"Half starved? Then how about a kiss to hold you over?"

She raised her eyes in surprise, feeling the thrill of anticipation already leaping up in the form of a blush. But he only pulled one of the paper-wrapped candy kisses from his pocket, and held it between index and middle fingers, offering it to Allison.

Their eyes met above it as they continued along the sidewalk. Her heart suddenly felt as if spring were burgeoning within it as well as in the apple, myrtle, and plum trees along the Madison streets.

"Oh, is that all?" she asked impishly. She plucked the candy from his fingers, opened it, and popped it into her mouth.

It seemed preordained that he drive again. "Where to?" he inquired, nosing the van into the busy end-of-the-day traffic near the Capitol.

"Back the way we came. There are plenty of cut-rate motels out that way." Without another word he headed out to Washington Avenue.

They entered the lobby of the Excel Motel together, each of them signing the register separately, ignoring the assessing glances cast their way by the clerk who asked, "Smoking or nonsmoking?"

Rick and Allison gaped at each other, then at the clerk.

"What?" they asked in unison.

"We got smoking rooms and nonsmoking rooms. Which one you want?"

"Nonsmoking," they answered, again in unison, and the clerk let his eyes drift from Allison to Rick as if to say, separate rooms, huh? He picked two keys from the wall, dropped them on the desk, and said, "Enjoy your stay."

On their way to the van—obviously the only vehicle parked out front, obviously the vehicle in which they had arrived together, obviously the vehicle which would take them to door C and rooms 239 and 240—Allison could feel the clerk's eyes following them.

"Do you think he believed us?" Rick asked, casting her a sidelong glance.

"Not after we both spouted out 'Nonsmoking.' Have you ever heard of such a thing before?"

"Never."

"Me neither."

They climbed into the van, and Allison couldn't resist wagging two fingers at the desk clerk as they pulled away from the sidewalk—shades of the night watchman in days past.

In the hall, standing between the two assigned doors that were exactly opposite each other, Rick asked, "Which one do you want?"

"Where's east?"

"That way." He pointed to 240.

"Then that one. I like the sun in the morning."

"Two-forty, milady," he said with a slight bow from the waist after he'd opened the door and dropped the key into her palm. She stepped uncertainly inside. It was vaguely creepy going into the motel room alone. She poked her nose around the corner to eye the double bed, the floor, the closed draperies, then glanced over her shoulder to find Rick standing in the open doorway to his room, watching her.

"How's yours?" he asked.

LaVYRLE SPENCER

She shivered and shrugged. "Cold."

"There's probably a heater they leave turned off until guests are in. Just a minute." He hung up his clothing bag on the rack in his closet and crossed the hall, moving into her room without apparent self-consciousness, while she felt as if every eye in Madison, Wisconsin, was somehow watching them on closed-circuit TV. He bent to the heater on the wall and studied its dials. Abruptly he stood up. "Nope, that's just for air." He came toward her, and she stood as if rooted to the floor. "Excuse me," he said, taking her by the elbows to move her aside to adjust the thermostat behind her.

"There, it'll warm up in a minute. Everything else okay?"

"Sure, thanks." But suddenly she didn't want him to go back across the hall. The room seemed too impersonal and quiet, a queer, lonely place when she faced it alone.

Rick paused in the doorway. "Would it be all right if we didn't go to dinner right away? I thought I'd lie down awhile and catch a nap. It was a long drive. Maybe you should do the same."

"I don't mind."

"What time then?"

She shrugged again, feeling more lost and lonely than ever, realizing he was, indeed, going to leave her and close himself away in his own room. She wondered despondently if nothing more personal would come of the two days than candy kisses.

After all, she had been the one to give the May basket; the next move was up to him.

"Sixish?" she suggested now, her spirits definitely flattened.

"Six it is." He tossed up his room key, caught it, winked at her, and said, "Pick you up at your place." Then he was gone, closing the door behind him.

Chapter
ELEVEN

ALLISON couldn't sleep. If the exhilaration of the day's workshops hadn't kept her awake, the butterflies in her stomach would have. She turned on the television and tried a cable station, but a horror movie was playing—hardly uplifting or relaxing. She flicked the TV off, flounced onto the bed, crossed her hands behind her head, and lay there like a ramrod.

Was he actually asleep over there while she lay here so keyed up over . . . over *everything* that it felt like she'd put a dime in the vibrator bed when she hadn't? How could he! The unsettled situation between them was as effective as any bottled stimulant on the druggist's shelves and getting more potent as the time for their "date" neared.

How should she act? As if she'd never shared a night of intimacy with Rick Lang that ended in near disaster? As if she had invited him to Madison, Wisconsin, solely to pose for her? As if she wasn't dying inside as each passing hour made her doubt she had the wherewithal to attract him as she once had?

By five o'clock her nerves were strung out like taut twine, and she ran a tub full of water—something she never did at home, it seemed sinful.

Sinking into bubbles up to her neck, she eased back, closing her eyes, willing herself to relax, be natural, just be her old full-of-piss-and-vinegar self. That was the girl he'd liked once. Crack a joke. Wear a smile. Banter. Tease.

But she felt like doing none of these. She felt like telling Rick Lang she loved him more than any man on the face of the earth, and if he didn't do something about it soon, she'd be a basket case.

She emerged from the bath wrinkled like a prune, having discovered that she had actually managed to fall asleep when she hadn't meant to. It was twenty minutes to six!

Forsaking shampoo, she settled for a quick recurling job with the hot iron, her usual light makeup, slightly heavier on the mascara for evening wear and a deeper shade of lipstick, almost umber, which shone like quicksilver when she checked her reflection in the mirror.

Cologne! She checked her watch—four minutes left. Rummaging through her bag, she came up with her favorite perfume and spared no immodesty, lavishing it on every intimate part of her body.

A knock on the door!

Oh Lord! He was two minutes early and she didn't have her dress on yet!

She flew to the coat rack, tore the yellow two-piece suit off the hanger, and clambered into the skirt, snatching a white eyelet blouse, trying to button up both at once.

He knocked again and called through the door, "Allison, are you awake?"

Her fingers seemed to be made of Silly Putty as she buttoned the minuscule pearl buttons of the blouse, which were round and insisted on slipping out of the holes nearly as fast as they went in.

"Allison?"

She yanked open the door, stopping his knuckles in midair as he raised them to rap again. For the second time that day his appearance brought her to a dead halt. This time he was dressed in an extremely formal vested suit of cocoa brown with an off-white shirt and Windsor-knotted tie in complementary stripes. The sight of Rick Lang in such clothing took Allison's breath away.

Her cheeks were as pink as crabapple blossoms, her hair lying in soft feathery ruff about her shoulders. His eyes traveled downward. Her hands were behind her back, closing the button on her skirt, and the strain at the front of the blouse made the top button pop open. His eyes moved lower to her feet, in nylons but no shoes. He cocked an eyebrow.

"Everything went wrong . . . I'm sorry," she wailed.

Dark, smiling eyes moved back to hers. "There's not a thing wrong with what I can see."

"I tried to sleep, but I couldn't. So I decided to take a bath, then fell asleep in the tub, of all things. And when I woke up it was nearly twenty to six already!" She turned away to rummage through her suitcase, coming up with high spike heels, all black patent-leather straps. He watched, fascinated, as she leaned to brace a hand on the bed, her back to him while she slipped the sling-back pumps on one shapely heel, then the other. It was the first time he'd ever seen her in a skirt. Her legs were thin but curved, and from behind, in the flattering shoes, they totally captivated Rick's eyes, which traveled up their shapely length to the enticing curve of her derrière as she leaned over, working on the second shoe.

He saw her check her bodice, then rebutton the top

button of her blouse, her back still toward him. Leaning over her suitcase, she took out something from a tiny white box, raised her elbows, and fastened it about her neck. The scent she'd put on was everywhere in the room, and as she lifted her graceful elbows, it filled his nostrils, mesmerizing him, just as he was mesmerized by the sight of her adding these last feminine touches.

She turned. A tiny gold heart hung from a delicate chain in the hollow of her throat. The vanity mirror was just beside the door where Rick stood. She moved toward it while his eyes followed. Her bewildering, powdery scent became headier as she neared him, leaned over the vanity toward the mirror, and put tiny gold hoop earrings into her pierced ears. His eyes traveled down to where she bent at the hip. When he looked up he found Allison watching him while she put the back on the second earring. Once more the top button of her blouse had come undone. He followed her fingers in the mirror as they closed it yet again.

From the coat rack she took a yellow long-sleeved jacket that matched her skirt. He crossed the short expanse to her side, and when she turned, Allison found him at her shoulder.

"I'll trade you," he said, producing from behind his back a single long-stemmed red rose that suddenly seemed to be reflected in her cheeks as her startled eyes caressed it.

It occurred to Allison that while she was deriding him for calmly napping, he'd been out buying the flower. Wordlessly she took it, relinquishing the jacket to his waiting hands, closing her eyes, and breathing deeply of the flower's fragrance while her back was turned, and he assisted her into the jacket.

When she faced him again, she held the stem of the rose in both hands, looking down at it, then up into his eyes. "Rick, I don't deserve this." Tears suddenly burned her eyes. "Oh God, Rick, I'm so sorry."

His face was somber. He did not touch her. "I'm sorry, too."

"You have nothing to apologize for. I . . . I hurt you so badly. I was so unfair . . . I know that now."

"Allison, you weren't ready. You tried to tell me that, but I wouldn't listen."

"No, Rick, I was such a damn fool. But I had some growing up to do, some sorting out. I was mixed up and angry and unsure."

"And how are you now?"

She didn't know what to say, was afraid to admit how totally committed she'd become to making up everything to him, to letting their relationship thrive. If only he'd touch her, give her some clue to his feelings.

"I'm . . . I'm sorted out, and no longer angry, and sure." Touch me, hold me, tell me I'm forgiven, her heart cried.

But his touch was only a brief pat on her elbow.

"Let's talk about it after dinner." He took her elbow and guided her out the door, down the hall, and into the brisk May evening.

He drove to a restaurant called the Speakeasy where the waiters wore striped shirts and arm bands and parted their hair down the middle. But neither Allison nor Rick really noticed.

The menus were the size of billboards. Still Rick managed to study her over his. She looked up. The candle put lights into his eyes, color in his cheeks, and shadows about his lips, which still did not smile. Studying his somber face, Allison wondered again what he would say if she simply told him the truth that ached to be spoken.

I love you, Rick Lang. I want you in my bed. I want you in my life.

The waiter approached, tugging her back to earth.

While they waited for swordfish and well-done filet mignon, the wine steward brought wine, flamboyantly exercising his skill in removing the cork, testing the bouquet, pouring, and offering a sample for Rick's approval.

Rick tasted, nodded. The steward filled two glasses and faded away.

"How did I do? Was I convincing?" Rick asked.

"Very." She brightened falsely. "I'd have sworn you were a connoisseur of . . ." She checked the label on the bottle, but could not pronounce it.

"Moonshine '82," Rick filled in, and they laughed at their ignorance. But the gay mood was forced.

"And I've never known anyone who ate filet well-done. Did you see the scowl the waiter gave you?"

She shrugged. "I feel rare enough tonight without rare steak, too."

He leaned forward, bracing tailored sleeves on the edge of the table, blue eyes moving over hers. "Do you? Do you really?"

"Yes, I do . . . really."

He lifted his glass in a toast. "Then here's to a rare night."

They drank, less of the wine than of each other across the tops of their glasses. Resting his footed goblet upon the linen cloth, Rick made small circles with it, studying it momentarily before his hand fell still and he watched her face as flickering candlelight changed its dancing shadows. Silently he reached, laid his hand, palm up, on the tabletop.

Her eyes flickered to it, then back to his, cautiously.

"Allison, if I don't touch you soon, I'm going to go crazy," he said quietly, only the hand reaching, the rest of him leaning back with casual grace, ankle crossed over knee as if he'd only said, "Allison, the temperature outside is seventy-two degrees," while every atom in her body went into motion until she felt explosive.

"Oh God, me too." She slid her palm over his and he

slowly closed his fingers until they were squeezing hers so tightly she thought her bones would break. He began moving his thumb, brushing it lightly across the backs of her knuckles as she sat stricken speechless, overwhelmed by the sensations that just his thumb could create within her body. She stared at their joined hands, wondering if he could feel the throbbing of her heart in her fingertips as she could.

"Do you dance?" he inquired quietly.

"Not very well."

"Me either, but I will if you will."

As they got to their feet the waiter brought Caesar salad. They turned toward the stamp-sized dance floor instead, where a man with an amiable smile played *Misty* on the piano.

Allison turned into Rick's arms, the two of them the only ones on the floor, neither even aware of it as his arm circled her waist and she moved near, resting her temple lightly against his jaw, her palm on his shoulder. Their movements were more of a gentle, unconscious sway than a dance, for they had not come here to dance, but to touch.

His aftershave was faint, spicy, the shoulder of his suit coat firm and cool. The piano player began singing softly in a soulful voice, "Look at me, I'm as helpless as a kitten up a tree . . ." He smiled as he watched the handsome blond man wrap both arms around the tall, striking woman, and hers move up to circle his neck.

Rick rested his joined hands lightly on the hollow of Allison's spine, while his head dropped down and hers lifted. The words of the haunting old Erroll Garner song drifted about Allison, and she did feel helpless, clinging to a cloud, misty. Her hips rested lightly against Rick's, and the touch of his hands on the hollow of her spine sent shivers coursing upward. They moved in indolent swaying steps that took them nowhere but heaven as their thighs brushed and he leaned his forehead down to rest it on hers.

"I love you, Allison Scott, you know that, don't you?" he whispered.

She pulled back only far enough to see his face, while the beginning words of the song reverberated through her body, ringing now with triumph—*Look at me! Look at me! Look at me! Rick Lang just said he loves me!*

Her voice trembled and her eyes sparkled as she admitted, "Yes . . . I know." She lay her fingertips on the back of his neck, above his collar—she suddenly had to touch his bare skin. "I love you, too, Rick Lang, you know that, don't you?"

"I've had my suspicions, but you put me through hell making me believe it."

"But you do?"

"I want to."

"Then do, because it's true."

He reached behind his neck to capture her right hand and reverted to the traditional waltz position. Her temple was again beside his ear. "Will you do something for me?" he asked.

"Anything."

"Maybe you shouldn't be so quick to answer 'anything.' This may be tough."

"Anything."

Again he stepped back and looked into her eyes. "Tell me about Jason."

Her steps faltered, a brief glint of uncertainty flickered in her eyes, but just then the music ended. He took her elbow and led her away from the floor. She watched the tips of her toes as they made their way back to the table. As Rick pulled her chair out, she felt a momentary sense of panic, then he was across from her, reaching for her hand again.

"Allison, you've just told me you love me. Will you trust me enough to tell me about Jason—everything, so his ghost will be exorcised? And this time without anger. If you can talk about him without anger, I'll know you're free of him at last, and ready for what you and I . . . well, just ready."

Wide brown eyes flickered to Rick's, then to the flame of the candle.

"Tell me . . . all of it."

She began softly. "He was my favorite, wonderful, sensational model. But first and foremost, he was a hedonist, only I never realized it until he'd left me." Tears glimmered in her eyes. She swallowed, pulling her hand from Rick's to hide her face. "Oh God," she said to the tabletop, "I don't know how to tell it. I was such a fool."

"Give me your hand," he ordered gently, "and don't look away from me."

She drew a deep, shuddering sigh as she began again, her hand in Rick's. She told him everything, how she'd begun by taking Jason's photo, then accepted the idea of his moving in; how she'd paid all the bills; how he'd used his body to get her to close her eyes to his shortcomings and character faults; how they'd collected the portfolio of photos; how he'd stolen them; even about his signature on the easel picture. She laughed sadly, softly, looking up into Rick's eyes. "And you know what?" Strangely, it hurt hardly at all to admit, "It was the only time he ever mentioned the word love."

Allison glanced at the wine bottle. "Could I have a little more of that?"

Rick released her hand. "No. You don't need it. Eat your salad while you finish. It'll take away the hollow feeling until I can."

Again she met his eyes, which did not smile or make

light of his words. Neither did they denigrate her for the past she'd just revealed so blatantly. She sighed deeply and ate her salad.

THE night was damp and cool, but scented with golden mock orange and lilac in full bloom. They walked with measured steps, Allison matching hers to Rick's as they crossed the parking lot to the door of the motel. She was tucked securely against his hip, wishing he'd walk faster. But he sauntered with torturous slowness, lugging the heavy glass door open without relinquishing his hold on her, laughing with Allison as they struggled inside, two abreast, bruising their hips.

They took the stairs in unison, eagerness growing with each step. Halfway up he stopped.

"I can't wait any longer." His arm swept around her and forced her back against the handrail as he gave her a taste of what lay in store. The sweet intoxication of his lips made her head spin.

"You keep that up and I'll be lying bruised and broken at the bottom of these steps, Mr. Lang. Don't you know better than to make a lady dizzy halfway up a flight of stairs?"

"I beg your pardon, Miss Scott. Common sense seems to have fled."

She pulled his head down to hers and mumbled against his mouth, "Oh, goody."

In the hallway between their two doors he asked simply, "My room or yours?"

"Tell me, Mr. Lang," she asked piquantly, arms looped about his neck, head tilted to one side, "do you like the sun in the morning?"

"I love the sun in the morning."

"Then mine."

She produced her key, handed it to him, and when the door swung wide open they stood for a moment studying each other, the smiles gone from their faces.

"I feel it only fair to warn you," he said, "that I've never before told a woman I love her before I made love to her."

"And how about after?"

"No, Allison, not even after."

"Supposing you don't after . . . well, after this one." Her eyes skittered down to her nervous fingers, then back up to his. "Just forget what I said one time about forsaking all others, okay? I'm . . . heck, I'm fifty years behind the times."

"Allison, I—"

"Shh." She covered his lips with her fingertips. "Just kiss me, Rick, hold me, and let's start starting over."

His palms molded her face, lifting it to receive his

kiss, which spoke of an ardency that drove all memory of the past from her mind. With their lips still joined, they moved inside her room. He caught the door with his heel, and when it slammed they fell against it, lost in each other's arms.

"Allison, I'll never hurt you, never knowingly," he promised in a gruff voice. "That other time when I thought I had . . ." He swallowed, pinning her tightly against the length of his body, clasping her head against his chest. "Please, darling, just be honest with me, always."

"I promise," she vowed as she kissed the side of his neck, then pressed her forehead against it, feeling the thrum of his heart there momentarily before backing out of his embrace and looking into his eyes while she slowly, methodically began removing her clothes.

As her jacket came off, his hands were still. As she reached for the button at the back of her skirt, he slowly, slowly began tugging the knot from his tie. They watched each other remove article by article until she stood before him in half-slip, panties and bra. Then he ordered, "Stop . . . let me."

Her hands fell still as he reached for the clasp of her bra. He was barefooted, only trousers and shirt still on, the latter pulled out of his waistband, hanging open to reveal the bare skin of his chest underneath.

Her suitcase lay open on the bed. In one motion he

closed it and swept it to the floor, then flipped the covers down over the foot of the mattress.

He tugged her to the bed, urging her down until they lay facing each other, his hand on the bare band of skin above her slip. As his face moved over hers, blocking out the light from the bedside lamp, her eyes closed. Soft, seeking kisses urged her trembling lips to open. Warm, gentle palms encouraged her back to relax. Hard, golden arms prompted her hips to move closer. And when they had, the rapture began. He mastered her hesitation by again moving with a slow hand, at first only the heel of it slipping to the side of her breast, brushing against the silky fabric that covered it, pressing, caressing, yet at a lazy pace that lulled and suggested and made her want more. He explored her back with a widespread hand, sliding down over the shallows of her spine, making the silken fabric of the half-slip seduce her skin before easing his fingers inside its elastic to let his flesh take its place. And so he pressed her womanly core hard against his swollen body, moving rhythmically against her until her hands began moving up and down his shirt, then inside, against the warm skin of his back.

"Oh, how I missed you, missed you," Allison whispered greedily.

"I missed you, too, every day, every minute."

His tongue danced desirously upon hers, and she

slipped her hands over his arms, until he shrugged out of the shirt, and it lay forgotten beneath him. He cupped her breast fully, pushing it upward to forcibly change its shape as he lowered his head and ran his tongue just above the transparent lily-shaped lace that edged her bra, revealing the dark, dusky nipple behind it. She dropped back, soft sounds coming from her throat, her eyes drifting closed as he leaned across her body and continued kissing only the tops of her breasts. There was a sweet yearning pain in her tightly gathered nipples that only his mouth could calm.

She arched off the mattress in invitation, and his hands slipped behind to release the clasp of the bra. She opened her eyes to watch his blond head dip once again to her naked skin and shuddered when his wet tongue touched, tempted.

Her hands blindly sought his body, skimming from chest to hard belly, then lower, caressing, cupping, inciting his breath to beat rapidly against her skin.

She pushed him up and away, the better to reach, and he fell back, tense, waiting, his eyes closed and nostrils flaring while she sat beside him, leaning back on one palm as she watched her hand play over him. His chest rose and fell with a driving beat while he lay, wrists up, drifting in pleasure. She released the hidden hook on the waistband of his trousers, then unzipped them, feeling his hand brushing softly against her back, though he lay as before, eyes closed, only that hand in motion.

There was nothing to equal the sense of celebration she knew as she undressed him fully, brushing his clothing away until he lay naked, golden brown, flat bellied, aroused, silent, waiting. She touched him, and he jerked once as if a jolt of electricity had sizzled through him, lifting his back momentarily off the bed. Then he lay as before, his fingertips lightly grazing her back while she stroked his bare leg, from inner thigh to sharp-boned knee that bent over the edge of the mattress.

"I love you so much," she uttered. And without compunction she captured his heat in her hand, leaned over, and kissed it briefly. "You're so beautiful."

"Allison, darling, come here." He tugged at her elbow, and she fell back beside him. "It's inside that I want to be beautiful for you. It's an accident if what you see is beautiful. But for you I want to have a beautiful soul . . . like yours is to me." His eyes were eloquent as he spoke into hers.

"Rick, I love you . . . I love you . . . body, soul, inside, outside. How could I ever have thought you were like him?" She clung to his neck, kissing his jaw, cheek, the corner of his mouth, then opened her lips beneath his to let him delve into the wet silk of her mouth.

His body was quivering as he pulled away. "Hey, where did you learn what you did a minute ago?"

"I told you, Jason was a hedonist. He had no compunctions about making his wishes known. He reveled in it."

"And that's why the song triggered your panic that night we were making love?"

"Yes."

He kissed the hollow just beneath her lower lip, speaking against her skin, his words rough-edged with passion. "I only take as good as I give, Allison, and with me it's ladies first, okay?"

Her answer was one of silent language, spoken with lithe limb and straining muscle, with wet tongue and willing skin. He shimmered the remaining garments down her legs, leaving her clothed in nothing but a tiny gold heart in the hollow of her throat. From there his lips began their downward journey. They traveled her body at will, tasting desire in its every quiver and shiver. He kissed her stomach, the soft valleys beside hip, behind knees, her ankles, thighs, lost in the fragrance he'd once watched her apply to secret, hidden places.

"I love you, Allison . . . beautiful Allison," he murmured and lifted himself above her, poised on the brink of a beauty surpassing the visual. And a moment later their bodies became one.

During the minutes that followed, stroking her to climax, he gave her the sense of self each being must have before giving that self to another, unfettered. It had been taken from her by another, in an eon far removed from now, but was returned in all its glory by this man Allison Scott had finally come to trust.

WHEN they lay exhausted, damp and disheveled in a faultless disarray, limbs languid and lifeless, apart from each other yet knowing they would never truly be apart, he ran a bare sole along her calf. "Now who turns you on more, me or my Hasselblad?"

Her voice came lazily from two feet away. "Right now, my darling Richard, ain't no way you could turn me on. I done been turned till I can't turn no more."

A replete chuckle came from his side of the bed, then a lethargic hand flopped down wherever it happened to flop. It landed on her ribs, felt around, discovered its whereabouts and rectified the mistake.

"Oh yeah? Want me to prove differently?"

She swatted the hand away, but it returned promptly, along with another to gather her against his long, naked body before he yanked the blankets up to cover them.

"I was shivering, that's why they were puckered up."

"Oh, and here all this time I thought it was the mention of my Hasselblad that did it."

"Oh, that too."

"Anything else?"

They were snuggled so close a bedbug couldn't have crawled between them.

"Nothing comes to mind."

"Nothing?"

She reached beneath the covers while she teased, "Not one eentsy-weentsy little thing."

He yanked her hand up and pinned both wrists over her head, laying across her chest. "That, you little snot, was a low blow. Just for that I may not suggest what I was just on the verge of suggesting when your sharp little tongue did you out of something you'd sell your soul for."

She struggled to lift her head to rain kisses of apology and giggling persuasion on his chin, nose, and mouth, but he backed far enough away that she couldn't reach.

"I take it back," she promised. "Especially since I know it's only temporary."

"Hey, lady, you want my Hasselblad for life, or don't you?"

"Do you come along with it?"

The pressure on her wrists disappeared. His lips swept down toward hers, a suggestive glint in his eyes as he answered, "You're damn right."

"For life?" she inquired. "For honest-to-goodness life?"

"For life."

"Forsaking all others?"

"Forsaking all others."

And ten minutes later she sold her soul for the second time that night.

From the New York Times bestselling author
LaVyrle Spencer